RETURN TO PEAKS ISLAND

BY: JOSH SCANDLEN

Table of Contents

Acknowledgements

God is good, always, and at all times. May I never forget that.

John McLaughin for allowing me to use one of his fantastic pictures for the cover of this book. You can find his work here at Flickr.

My wife and my four kids for keeping me young. Being a husband and dad is simply the best thing ever.

The friends I've met on my youtube channel for their continued support.

My mom, sister and brother for editing this piece of work and steering me in the right direction. I shudder to think what I might have published if they didn't take the time for commentary.

My dad - Young men learn a lot from their father's. I am profoundly grateful for the lessons I learned from him.

Peaks Island, Maine -
It's funny actually because for many years, when I was younger and had moved away, I tried to 'escape' my being a native of not just Maine but having been

raised on a tiny island. It was embarrassing to say you were from a place where nothing was happening except to watch the snow.

As I aged though and raised my own kids in suburban settings, I have come to realize how awesome I had it as a kid growing up on Peaks. Very few people will ever know what it's like to take a boat to school, for instance. And I'm one of 'em. How cool is that?

At the same time the turbulent and revolutionary fervor of the later Sixties had its impact. Hippies migrated from as far away as Haight Ashbury to settle Peaks. " We didn't have all that many here, and they didn't stay long. There was nothing here for them, " says John Feeny.

The Seventies brought stagnation, but also the return of a certain composure as the former "community life" of earlier times took hold.

With the dawning of the high strung and affluent Eighties, a new generation evolved. A new breed of young urban professionals or yuppies appeared and transformed Peaks into a chic, trendy real estate target.

The end of the Eighties brings the slow fade of high times. For Peaks it's the end of an era that has brought gentrification to its real estate and yuppies to its shores. Times are changing and Peaks Island, by no means a stagnant time capsule, changes with it.

Until lately, when professionals from New York or Boston got the urge to flee the rat race and move to Maine, they generally became carpenters or boat builders. But today, with these new technologies at hand, latterday dropouts can just as easily continue with their white-collar professions and their white-collar salaries while living a more congenial life.

Maine

There is nothing like September and October in Maine. The beauty of the fall makes the winters almost bearable. Nothing is as majestic as the deep red, orange and yellow leaves of the deciduous trees underneath a cobalt blue sky.

The sun seems to tilt in a way which magnifies how it lights up the land, drawing out the natural colors so much they actually seem to speak. Maybe only natives hear it but they communicate to your very soul, reminding you of your existence as a part of a beautiful, living world.

Then the cool breeze settles in and gently rubs you on your shoulder. It's not a full embrace, mind you. Not like a warm summer wind that gathers you in a bear hug. This is more a touching reminder that winter is coming and to get prepared, like an alarm clock that starts off calmly but begins to shriek the longer you wait to turn it off. In September, the wind whispers. Come the end of October though, it's in full blown panic, screaming that the dark of winter is coming. Prepare! Prepare! Prepare!

Tourists to Maine who have yet to experience a winter don't get it. They see the beauty, feel the cool breeze and smell the wood stove fires of people heating their homes. They think it's just the natural progression of living in a state with four seasons. Oh, but how wrong they are. Yes, there are four seasons in Maine. But winter is the most dominant. From mid-October through the end of March, the winter engages in full ferocity. A few weeks of fall are all the warning you get about winter's inevitable arrival. When fall emerges, those in the know take precautions. They know what is coming and they don't want to be caught unprepared. Many newcomers find that after a winter or two they can't take it and move back to wherever they came from.

Even many natives grow weary of the fight. They flee to the literal greener pastures down South. But what they don't know, as they devise their escape plans, is that while they can physically leave Maine, Maine never leaves them. It's always calling out, reminding them of "The Way Life Is Meant To Be". Are the long commutes, the insufferable rat race, the spoiled air quality, worth having a few less weeks of winter?

"The Way Life Is Meant To Be" can bring a desire for natives to go back. Sometimes that longing is nothing but a fantasy. Other times though, it's almost as if they are being called to return, like some magnetic force is pulling them back to the state of Maine. Which is exactly what happened to Rob McKenzie.

Part I

Working Late

"Working late…again?" and then the long pause as Sandy's voice trailed off.

"Sandy," Rob said exasperatingly into the phone. Seemed they had this discussion every night. "If I don't make the money we can't live like how you want. I know you *know* this."

"Can't live like how *I* want? *I'm* not the one with the new Tesla, Rob! *I'm* not the one who wants a vacation home. Don't blame me for *your* spending problems." Sandy paused and Rob said nothing. Then she continued.

"What is it with you anyway, with needing a new vehicle and vacation home? Someone you're trying to impress?"

"Sandy, don't be silly. Who would I be trying to impress?"

"Come on, Rob. I know you've been out to lunch on more than one occasion with Lisa. Did you really think I wouldn't find out?"

"Wha-?" Rob was stunned. How did she know? "Oh, so now you're spying on me, Sandy?" He asked, sounding much more defensive than he meant to.

If you accuse your spouse of spying on you that means you know you were up to no good. Think about it.

If you were going to lunch with, say, Jimmy, and your wife asked you about it, you wouldn't accuse her of spying. You'd simply say, "yeah, Jimmy and I needed to go over some stuff and figured we might as well eat while doing it." But the fact Rob was so defensive was a sure sign something was up.

"So you're not denying it, Rob?" Sandy asked, seeming to mock him.

Rob knew he was beaten. Sandy was more nimble than Rob and it frustrated him. She always got the best of him in these arguments. This time it was more than just a run-of-the-mill argument, though. Rob *had* been going to lunch with Lisa from the office. It was becoming somewhat intimate too. No kissing or anything, *yet*, but there was a growing energy.

"Why would I deny it, Sandy? I have lunch with people from the office all the time." Rob stated, trying to sound matter of fact. But the damage was done.

Sandy didn't need to say anything more. No, she was too good for that. She didn't even need to give Rob the silent treatment she had perfected over their years together. This time she dropped the mother-of-all-bombs on Rob; She just laughed and hung up the phone.

New Money

Rob's childhood, well, it was complicated. Some young men in their late teens are not mature and tend to find trouble and Rob found more than his fair share. He was fortunate to even graduate high school. In his first real instance of maturity, realizing he had limited prospects, he enlisted in the Army.

A four year tour did for Rob what it does for many young men, straightened him out. After he was discharged he went on to college paid for by the taxpayer. Turns out he was a pretty good student. He actually enjoyed learning, something that no one would accuse him of in his high school years. Upon graduating he was offered a great-paying job with a start-up in the emerging IT field.

Rob's company grew beyond all expectations and he rode the wave with it. In just a couple years, he was Senior Vice President of Sales and Rob and Sandy had money for the first time in either of their lives. It was amazing being able to take a vacation, pay cash for it and not have a credit card bill hanging over their heads.

It was even more amazing at how quickly they were able to adjust to having money. When they first started out, they lived in a lower middle class neighborhood where everyone drove older vehicles and lived in ranch-style homes. Many neighbors didn't even have garages. In fact, for Rob and Sandy the idea of a paved driveway was a "must-be-nice" goal. Later though, after buying a beautiful house in a gated, golf community with an expensive country club membership, a $200,000 landscape renovation was a must-have.

To pay for their increasing consumption, Rob spent long hours at work and less at home. Many nights he'd get home not only after dinner but even after the kids were in bed.

Rob seemed more married to his job than to the family and Sandy became resentful. She started to go shopping and spend money to fill the void left by his absence. She also began to hang around with the other neighborhood ladies who spent their afternoons at the country club. Sometimes they played golf or tennis, but mostly they just lounged at the pool, sipping on cocktails while their kids were at school. Not often, but every now and again, the kids would come home to find Sandy passed out on the couch.

More and more Sandy had even taken to staying at the country club past dinner and the kids would have nothing prepared to eat. Rob, of course, wasn't at home either as he was at the office making the money for Sandy to spend. Well, that's what he told himself, forgetting about that $100,000 Tesla he drove.

The kids would call telling him that mom wasn't home and there was no dinner. Rob would order something to be delivered and then call Sandy to tell her the kids had nothing to eat. Invariably she'd answer and, with a rather boisterous crowd in the background, stumble over her words.

"The kids don't have dinner, Sandy," Rob would chastise her.

"Why don't you make something for them then!" she'd shout at Rob.

"I'm at work, Sandy!" Rob would say, getting frustrated. The same childish argument almost daily now it seemed. "The kids need to eat. You have to stop putting your club friends before the kids, Sandy!"

So damn exasperating. Is she doing this just to spite me? Rob wondered. It's like she's holding the kids hostage just to get under my skin.

"Says the guy who is never home for a family dinner because he's got a girlfriend at the office!" Sandy responded. "Why don't *you* stop putting work before the kids, or *me*, Rob!" Then she hung up.

Rob was convinced he wasn't putting work before the family though. The reason he was working so hard was *for* the family! Again, forgetting about his $100,000 Tesla.

Suddenly it hit him. The way she said "stop putting work before the kids '*or me*.'" It was like a Freudian slip. That was the first time she had ever let on that she was actually hurt by Rob's long work hours. It must have devastated her to find out he was spending a lot of time with another lady, be it under the guise of work or not. Obviously, Sandy would never state that explicitly, she had too much pride. But she said it.

Rob had placed his priority on work, and the people there, at the expense of his wife. How could he have not seen this before? Never mind the kids not having their father around for dinner on a regular basis. That's a given. But his very wife, his soulmate, needed his companionship too and he wasn't there to provide it. So she got it somewhere else, at the club with her friends there and who knew who else. What a fool he had been not to have seen this before!

Separation?

Marriages do fail. And it certainly seemed like theirs could too. But Rob wasn't about to lose his marriage over an office flirtation so he was going to try and make it right. He left work early in hopes to surprise Sandy by making dinner for the entire family.

He was in the bedroom changing out of his business attire when Sandy came in. "What are you doing home so early, Rob?" She asked, suspiciously.

"I'm gonna make dinner for the family so we can eat together for once. I want to make things right. I know I wasn't upfront about Lisa but nothing happened. I need you to believe me."

"Rob, I don't care. You can have a relationship with anyone you want, if that's what you want. If not, then don't. It's completely up to you."

Rob was floored. "What are you saying Sandy? We can start dating other people or something? Sandy, I know I've neglected you, and the kids, but I'm going to change."

"I'm doing just fine, Rob." Then added for emphasis, "*we're* doing fine. Not sure why you have this guilty conscience all of a sudden. Do you really think I'm upset because you were trying to hide your little office affair? You really don't get it do you? For years, I have been at home waiting for you. But your work was always more important. Now, only when I found out about this other lady, all of a sudden you value me and the kids. You certainly didn't seem to care much before though. So why should I care now?" And then she laughed. It was the laughter that hurt most. Laughter was the ultimate "I don't care." Anger, yelling, tears would have been better, anything but the laughter.

"So what's going to happen, Sandy?" Rob asked.

"What do you mean? Does something need to happen?"

"Well, we can't go on like this, can we? Living our own separate lives?"

Sandy burst out laughing even more. "Rob, where have you been??? We've been living separate lives for years! Why do we need to change now?"

Then she walked out of the room, down the stairs and out the door, presumably to hang out with her friends at the Country Club. How Rob hated that place and the people who went there. But he couldn't blame her. It was his absence that drove her there.

Was it Worth It?

Rob looked around at the luxury of his master bedroom. No corners were cut when they built this house. Exquisite design from one of the most sought-after architects in Phoenix. From the crown molding to the wainscoting and the fixtures, everything was top of the line. No expense spared. And this was just the bedroom. The downstairs was even more elegant.

Bored and lonely he headed to the living room where his boys were. They were buried in their phones and didn't even notice when he appeared.

"Hey guys," Rob said rather softly.

"Hey Dad," Connor, his oldest son, mumbled without looking away from his phone. Then he did a double take. "Dad? What are you doing here?"

It was only 5:30 pm and typically Rob wasn't home until the kids were in bed. Both boys looked up from their phones, almost startled to see their dad.

"Did you lose your job?" His youngest son, Jackson, asked.

Rob winced. "No, nothing like that. I just want to spend more time with you boys."

"Oh, allright," Jackson replied and then went right back to his phone.

"Anything you guys want to do?"

"Like what?" Connor asked.

"I don't know. You tell me."

"We're good, Dad." And right back to the phone.

Rob paused for a moment. Looked at his boys mesmerized by their phones, oblivious to his presence. "Okay, well if you think of anything just let me know." Neither boy responded.

He walked into the custom kitchen they had spent a fortune on. Rarely did he eat here as most of his meals were at the office and he wondered why he spent over a million dollars for a house he basically only used for sleeping? Maybe if they hadn't spent so much money on the house, and yes his Tesla too, he wouldn't have had to work so hard and could have been around more. Maybe if he was around more he would be in a better place with his family. Hindsight is always 20/20 but he couldn't escape the idea that where he was with Sandy now was nearly irreconcilable.

What have I done? What if Sandy has met someone else? What if it's over between us? Rob tried not to think like this. But the creeping despair was gathering, such a feeling of helplessness and there was nothing he could do. Sandy seemed to have moved on. Could Rob save the marriage? It didn't look like it.

Power is Seductive

With Sandy gone and the kids too immersed in their phones to barely acknowledge his existence, Rob figured he'd get some work done. He went to his home office and logged in remotely. Within seconds he had all the files he needed. He felt like kicking himself. Why wasn't he doing this before? He could have at least been home with the family for dinner.

Rob *knew* exactly why he spent long hours in the office, though. In the office, he *was* somebody; One of the bosses. People looked up to him, laughed at his jokes and made him feel important. Even the ladies in the office who normally would never have given him the time of day in any other environment listened to his every word.

Power is addictive. Having 20-something year old women fawn over you does a lot for self-esteem, especially compared to being at home when everything revolves around the kids. In the office though, you are king. And Rob had to admit, he loved that.

But the power trip stops outside of the office. Outside the office you're just another run-of-the-mill mid-career white collar chap. Nothing special. A bigger checkbook to buy more prestige if one needs to massage his ego but other than that no one cared.

Now, sitting in his home office, trying as he could, he couldn't concentrate on work. He was too depressed by how things were going at home. What a fool he'd been.

So to pass the time he browsed his social media feeds even though he knew what an absolute waste it was. The algorithms were designed to feed one's addiction to the "breaking news" that would generate a constant state of panic in users. It was called clickbait for a reason...because it worked.

He found himself looking at the wonderful lives of people he knew. Well, at least how wonderful they presented themselves. Rob wondered if the happiness they showed on social media was genuine or if they were hiding some of the same issues he was contending with.

He started looking at the pages of guys he served with in the Army. He even went back to some of the kids he was friends with in high school. Everyone is happy. The happiest families. The "Best Dad Ever". All that stuff. He knew it was fake. It had to be, right? He couldn't be the only one on the verge of a divorce, after all half of all marriages end in divorce.

Rob knew that statistic was bogus, though. Take out the people married more than once and actual divorce rates have dropped quite a bit. In fact, people who married in the 1990's, like Rob and Sandy, only have a 30% divorce rate. Focusing on the 50% number made Rob feel a little better though. "It's not just me…"

Then he came across a post reporting that Marcus Simone had died of suicide at the young age of forty-six.

Rob was shocked. Simone had been one of Rob's closest friends growing up on Peaks Island and to learn he died by suicide was stunning. Why did he, of all people, kill himself?

Why Go Hemingway?

Marcus Simone was an amazing story given where he started from. In tenth grade his family left Peaks Island to move to California. It was here where Marcus was exposed to computers for the first time. He immediately found his calling and in only a few short years, while still in his teens, made his first $100,000 designing video games from his bedroom. Three years later, at the age of twenty-one, he cracked a million and never looked back.

Marcus seemed to crave being a celebrity figure as well as being a tycoon. He was all over the news and the entertainment pages. He dated Hollywood actresses. Rubbed shoulders with the biggest celebrities. Hosted huge fundraisers for prominent politicians and charitable events. When it came to the Nouveau Riche and California glamor, Marcus Simone owned that space. Quite an impressive life for a kid from hardscrabble beginnings on Peaks Island

Marcus' suicide, a self-inflicted shotgun blast, captured national attention for a couple cycles. How could a guy at the epitome of his career with seemingly everything at his fingertips do this?

In just a few days' time, though, he was yesterday's news. The media moved on to the other horrible events that people love to consume and Marcus Simone was quickly forgotten.

This was personal for Rob, however. Marcus was his best friend growing up. Even though they hadn't spoken in decades, Marcus was enshrined in some of Rob's most cherished memories and Rob followed his career with satisfaction. It made him feel in some ways *he* too had arrived.

Rob wondered what the other kids he had grown up with on Peaks were thinking in regards to Marcus' suicide. Maybe some of them had kept in touch with him and had insight. He scoured social media trying to find any information or details about Marcus's death but found nothing.

Rob thought there would at least be some comments in the newspaper stories about Marcus. But even the newspapers in Maine paid little attention. The fact that a poor kid from Peaks Island who had become one of America's most successful glamor tycoons had suddenly killed himself would seem like a huge story for the folks in Maine. After all, how many Marcus Simone's were there from Maine? But after a couple news cycles it seemed Marcus Simone never even existed.

This made Rob realize that his own very existence, his actual stamp on the world, would be nothing too. No one remembers the nice house a suburban upper middle class man has when he dies. Or the cars. Or the value of a 401k.

When Rob died the only thing that would live on were the human beings he impacted. Seeing how his own sons barely acknowledged him, apparently he hadn't made much of an impact on anyone. If anyone remembered him at all it would be as just another guy who devoted more time to his work than his family.

He turned off his computer and sat back in his chair staring up at the ceiling, "let this be a lesson," he thought as he drifted off to sleep.

Dreaming

He was a kid again, all of eight or nine years old, riding his bike through the Back Shore of Peaks Island with Doggie, his creamsicle-colored dog and his best friend growing up. It was early morning and the sun was rising just above the ocean, inviting Rob to enjoy the adventures of the day. Oh how Rob loved when that sun winked at him early in the morning.

A sunny summer day in Maine meant freedom. He could do whatever he wanted. Explore the woods till his heart's content. Join a pick-up game of baseball with the other island kids. Go down to the wharf and jump into the swells of the boats as they pulled away. It was all his. When it rained, though, man, what a disappointment. Confined inside the house with nothing to do. Such a waste for a boy on summer vacation when days of independence were few.

He parked his bike in the bushes along Seashore Ave and walked down a rocky trail to where the beach lay. As always, tiny Catnip Island sat lazily about five hundred feet in the ocean in front of him. It was really nothing more than a pile of rocks with a strip of sand that pretended to be a beach; and only at low tide. The high tide waters would devour the beach and reduce the size of the "island" by half.

For Rob, Catnip Island existed for one reason and one reason only; to tease him, daring him to swim out to it. Other kids were able to swim out there and sometimes they'd be there for hours while Rob stayed behind, fearful and jealous. He worried if he attempted to swim out to it he'd tire before reaching it and someone would have to save him. If one of his friends had to rescue him, he would never recover from the humiliation, especially if there were girls around to witness it. One day, he always told himself he'd conquer Catnip island. Until that day, it would mock him mercilessly.

A thousand feet or so beyond Catnip Island were the spectacular cliffs of Cushing Island, a desolate place with only a few inhabitants living in houses passed down among generations. If one dared to venture past Cushing Island and veered off course just one degree, he wouldn't be seen again until he reached Puerto Rico in the south or France in the east.

It was the vastness of the ocean that always captured Rob in wonderment. Were there people sitting on the shores of France at this exact moment looking west as Rob looked east? Who were they? What was their story? Rob could sit there for hours just thinking of what lay beyond the waters that engulfed his tiny little island in the Casco Bay.

It was during these early morning moments that Rob knew he'd leave the island as soon as he could. He had to see what else was out there in the vast world. And

once he left, there was no way he'd ever come back. Or
so he thought.

Brackett Ave.

His dream suddenly changed and now he was no longer an eight year old boy at the beach with Doggie but was around eleven, standing on the wharf with Marcus Simone, their white and orange Portland Press Herald newspaper bags draped over their shoulders. Every afternoon at 4:35pm the boat would drop off a couple bundles of the Evening Express, the afternoon edition of Maine's largest paper, for Rob and Marcus to bring to the islanders who subscribed.

After the boat docked, the deckhand would toss the bundles onto the wharf. Rob and Marcus would secure them, flip them over and cut the plastic binder that held the papers together. They'd then load the newspapers into their bags and begin the trek across the island. They'd shuffle up the hill on Welch Street until they reached Island Ave where they'd split up. One would go north and the other south and they would meet in the middle after all the papers had been delivered. The next day they switched.

When the weather was good it'd take them no more than an hour and a half to go house-to-house putting newspapers in customer's requested spots, between the screen and the front door, in the mailbox, under a rock on the front porch, etc. Sometimes they'd have to fight off dogs to get the paper in the right place for the customer. Other times, a customer would get upset because they put the paper under the welcome mat when they specifically stated they wanted the paper someplace else. But all in all it wasn't a bad gig.

In the summertime it was more a hassle than anything because it took time away from doing other things they wanted to do. But when they got paid, it was well worth it. The money allowed them the freedom to buy whatever they wanted, mainly they'd use it for comic books, junk food and to play video games at Jones' Landing, the only place that served pizza on the island.

Bad weather changed everything. That's when the paper route became the worst job in the history of mankind. Brackett Avenue, which was by far the steepest road on the island, loomed like the Eye of Mordor, waiting for them. It ran right down the center of the island and was the only road that made it to both sides. Most of the houses were situated at the front part of Brackett Ave going up the hill. Where the road flattened the houses became further and further apart. In the summer, when you were wearing shorts and tennis shoes, it was a breeze to deliver the papers. Fewer houses meant fewer papers to deliver and less papers to carry. Usually the boy who had that as part of their route would finish first.

When the weather turned was when things became bad. Being such a long and steep road, it was a major chore getting up that hill while being decked out in full winter gear; Boots, gloves, hats, a heavy jacket. Not only were you carrying a sack of newspapers but it felt like you had another twenty pounds of clothing on while trudging through the snow, ice and wind blowing against you on the steepest road on the island.

Rob was also a bit creeped out by Brackett Ave, especially after a deep snow. While the bluish glow illuminated the surroundings, it felt like you were in the North Dakota badlands. There were no people out. No noises. No dogs outside. If a crazed person was out there, or a monster of some sort, now remember Rob was too old to believe in monsters, right? But let's just say *if* one were out there, there'd be no one to help him as everyone was inside, staying warm; Everyone but him of course. Rob was literally alone against the elements. Yeah, maybe he had an active imagination but delivering the papers up Brackett Ave during bad weather made the job nearly unbearable.

One cold, rainy and windy day, Rob and Marcus couldn't agree whose turn it was to deliver on Brackett Ave. They both insisted it was the other kid's turn to deliver up that hill. Rob felt he delivered up Brackett Ave way more times than Marcus did. Rob was so sure of it, he said he wasn't going to do it no matter what Marcus said.

Marcus argued he did it more and it was Rob's turn and he also said he wasn't going to do it either. They were at a stalemate as they stood there at the bottom of Brackett Ave arguing. Then things turned a bit nasty and, like when hockey players dropped their gloves, Rob and Marcus threw the paper bags from their shoulders and started punching and wrestling in the middle of the street.

The wind took advantage of the neglected newspaper bags and scattered the papers all over the intersection of Island and Brackett Aves. After the brief skirmish, the boys looked at the mess they caused and walked away in their separate directions, leaving the bags and newspapers all over the bottom of Brackett Ave.

Memories

Rob woke up, startled a bit. He looked around the room to make sure he was actually back in his home office. He'd never had a dream seem so real. "What the hell was that?" He wondered to himself. That dream was like he was there, literally reliving his past. He laughed as he remembered the fight he and Marcus got into while arguing who was going to deliver Brackett Ave.

He remembered another day when they didn't want to deliver the papers and decided to kick the bundles off the wharf into the water. Marcus counted down from three while Rob kicked the papers forward to the edge of the wharf. "Three!" Marcus yelled and Rob gently kicked the papers inching them forward. "Two!" and Rob did it again. "One!" and Rob gave a big kick this time sending the papers down to Davy Jones' locker, to which Marcus yelled "and they're gone!" Then they went on their merry way to enjoy the rest of the day.

At dinner, Rob received a call from his boss in Portland asking why the papers weren't delivered. Rob lied and said the boat didn't bring them. His boss laughed at Rob's obvious lie, he knew the boat delivered them. Then he told Rob he would withhold his pay as he himself was going to come out to personally make sure the papers were delivered that evening. Rob begged for his mom to intervene but she just smiled and said "I hope you learn a lesson."

"That's not fair," Rob whined. "He can't withhold my money!"

"Don't show up, don't get paid, Rob. It's that simple," Rob's mom answered.

Rob was flooded with memories of Marcus, like the time they got drunk before an 8th grade dance with a couple girls from Middle School and Rob threw up everywhere. And when they were Freshman at Portland High School and would skip class to go smoke cigarettes in the downtown Burger King. Also the time Marcus's uncle was having a party and Rob passed out drunk next to the toilet in the bathroom.

To say both Rob and Marcus as adults surpassed any expectations one would have had of them as kids would be the understatement of the year. Rob had become an affluent, upper middle class executive. Marcus, of course, was rich and world-famous. They overcame all obstacles thrown their way. And yet, Rob's marriage and family-life was falling apart and Marcus actually killed himself. How did it come to this?

Rob now found himself on a mission. He had to find out what happened to Marcus Simone. He needed to know more. He couldn't escape the fear that if a guy like Marcus Simone could just wake up one day and kill himself, that Rob could do the same. After all it seemed a divorce was becoming possible and he would no doubt lose custody of the kids. Could he deal with that? It scared him deeply. He decided to contact every kid he grew up with on Peaks Island to see if they had any information on what happened with Marcus. Maybe Marcus had mental issues? Maybe he was using? Rob needed to know.

Rachel DuBois

Because Peaks was such a small community when Rob lived there it didn't take long to reach out to the people he grew up with via social media. Oddly, most of the kids he grew up with had no social media presence at all, at least that he could find. Didn't *everyone* have a social media presence? Apparently not those from Maine.

Only one person, Rachel Dubois, responded when he reached out. No one else replied. Not even a "go to hell!" or a "I don't know who the hell you are!" Nothing. Dead silence. Except for Rachel. She even seemed to anticipate Rob contacting her and was eager to connect with him. Rob was wary. She and Rob never really knew each other growing up. Yes, they were in the same classes but that was it. They never spoke to each other, never hung out. But now she was telling Rob to come visit her on Peaks as she had lots of information to share with him.

This was just weird. Rob thought about dropping the whole thing and never looking back. Maybe Rachel had turned into a lonely cat lady looking for someone to talk to. After all, didn't you have to be kind of eccentric to live on an island year round? But Rob couldn't drop his investigation. He had to find out if anyone had more info on Marcus. It wasn't like he had much else to do anyway; His home life was falling apart. And the dream he had seemed to speak to him to get back to Peaks. When he told Sandy about Marcus' suicide and that he had a feeling he needed to get back for a few days to research why he did it, he thought she might be suspicious. But they were beyond that now. She just simply nodded her head and said "it's probably good we get a few days apart." Definitely not the send off Rob was hoping to hear.

Part II

Taxi Cab Driver

Rob's parents, Annie and Gerry, had moved to Maine from California to live a hippie, back-to-the-land lifestyle. They used up their savings to buy some land, site unseen, in Northern Maine to farm: A farm about as remote as one could get in the lower 48. They drove across the country in a run down pickup truck, sleeping in the bed and avoiding toll roads.

When they arrived in Maine, they found the land they purchased was nothing but rocks and not farmable. They got suckered. Unfortunately, they had no back up plan, nowhere to go and no money. Winter was approaching and they knew being homeless was not a viable option so they went to Portland, Maine's largest city, to figure things out. They rented a roach-infested one-bedroom apartment in a decaying part of the city. It was here when they found out they'd have an addition to the family, Rob.

With a baby on the way, they knew they couldn't stay in the slum with addicts passed out in the halls and dealers setting up shop outside the front entrance. So, Gerry took a job as a laborer shoveling snow on the docks during the day and drove a cab at night hoping to save enough money to move to a better apartment for when the baby arrived.

One night Gerry picked up a passenger who had stumbled his way out of a bar. In his drunken stupor, he told Gerry to hustle as he needed to get to the wharf to catch the last boat going back to Peaks.

"Miss that last boat and you're left sleeping on the wharf with the rats," the drunk said. "Not a pleasant way to spend a night. And trust me, I've spent many a-night there," he uttered, his head bobbing and his eyes barely staying open. Gerry worried this guy was going to pass out, or even worse, puke in the back seat which Gerry would have to clean.

"I've gotta get off that island," his passenger slurred. "Nothing is going on there and everyone's leaving. It was fun growing up but those days are over."

"Why? What's happening over there?" Gerry asked, trying to keep the man engaged so he wouldn't pass out.

"Would *you* want to live on an island, man?" Gerry's passenger responded, somewhat harshly. "There's nothing to do. The boats don't even run half the time. I'll be lucky if I get back tonight knowing how messed up the boat schedule is."

"I'll tell you though," he continued. "If you want to buy a cheap house, there are plenty on the island now. Hell, you can have my mom's," he laughed. "The only reason I'm still there is because my mom needs me and she insists on dying there. So, at least I get free rent. But

the minute she dies, man oh man, I'll take the first bid on
the house and leave that place forever."

Gerry was intrigued about the island thing. Cheap
houses? Well, that'd certainly be better than living in
their slum apartment with a kid on the way.

Cheap Houses

Turns out one indeed *could* get a house for cheap on the island. Just like the guy said, young adults were moving off to pursue more exciting lives elsewhere.

Boat transport was a major issue for island residents. Some days the boat only made a couple trips to Peaks Island or the other smaller islands in Casco Bay. Labor strife, mismanagement, drunken crew and the wharf itself was falling apart. No one had any incentive to get things to work smoothly which made getting to and from the island a constant challenge.

No jobs, no reliable transportation and the remoteness of island living reduced the year-round population to around 400 with many of the residents being senior citizens on Social Security and other government assistance. It was not a very appealing place for most people...except for the few who were trying to live a counterculture life, recluses, hippies and those who were not aligned with modern society, which was exactly what Gerry and Annie envisioned when they escaped California to move to Maine to begin with.

A winterized house on Peaks cost around $12,000 which was out of the price range for Gerry and Annie. A summer house, well, those you could get a whole lot cheaper because they were not built for people to live in during the harsh Maine winters.

Gerry found one summer home listed for $5,000. They had just enough to put $1,000 down and Annie's parents agreed to cosign for the mortgage for the remaining $4,000. The house did need a lot of work, insulation, a new roof, flooring, windows etc. Gerry was handy, though, and figured he could get everything updated before winter set in. Annie was apprehensive however.

"We have a baby on the way, Gerry!" She argued when first told of the "opportunity."

"Oh, I know. But, if we move now I can spend the summer working on the house so by winter it'll be fully winterized. And while I'm doing that you can work on the garden and raise chickens too," Gerry said excitedly. "This is what we've been waiting to do, Annie, live away from the city. Living on the island is the best thing we can do for our kids."

Annie was not so sure. Motherly instincts don't go away easily, after all.

"We can't live in a house that's freezing in the winter time, Gerry. What if we need to see a doctor? Do they have anyone on the island who can help us?" Annie retorted.

"Don't worry, honey. I'll get that place ready for winter," Gerry answered. "As for a doctor, I thought we

were going to raise our children without modern
medicine and be as natural as we could?"

Gerry was quite convincing because in two
weeks they closed on the $5,000 summer cottage and
used all the cash they had for the down payment. How
were they going to pay the mortgage? Well…that
remained to be seen.

Maggie and Jessica

Turns out winterizing a home on a rather remote island isn't as simple as Gerry thought, especially with hardly any money and no transportation. Getting materials to the island wasn't an easy task to begin with but it was nearly impossible without a vehicle. They sold the pickup truck they drove from California to raise the cash so they could move to the island.

By October, the baby, Rob, had arrived, and the winter cold came earlier than usual as the Global Cooling scare of the 1970's bore down. Winter days turn dark early in Maine, much earlier than Rob or Annie had ever experienced which was intimidating in of itself. The wind off the ocean creating cold drafts throughout the house concerned Annie even more.

"When are you going to be done with the renovation, Gerry? We're going to freeze this winter!"

Unfortunately, as the hours of daylight declined, Gerry's motivation to fix up the house did too. He was rapidly losing interest in the project he promised Annie he'd complete before winter set in. They were nearly out of money and Gerry didn't have a job so no money was coming in either. They had little food. No oil to heat the house. Even worse was that Gerry had met up with that same drunk passenger from when he drove the taxi, the guy who told him about the island to begin with. They quickly became drinking buddies. They would get together, drink and smoke dope when Gerry was supposed to be working on the house. Winter was approaching and things were not looking good. Gerry seemed oblivious though.

"Oh, don't worry, hun," he would tell Annie after coming home from a night of hanging out with his new friend. "We can heat the house with wood. There is a wood stove, after all."

"You realize the wood stove is in the dining room, right?" She snapped back. "So are we going to sleep there, in the dining room?"

"Awww, look hun. We'll be okay. Just trust me. It'll be okay," he said as he passed out on the couch.

Baby Rob was not happy either. He began to throw massive fits. He was hungry and cold. Annie didn't know what to do. She was a new mom and quite young. Rob's constant crying, the cold, the hunger and Gerry passing out night after night finally got to her. She knew she had to do something before the winter came.

One night while Gerry was out with his new friend, Annie bundled up Rob and left the house to find someone who could help her. She needed to use a phone so she could call her parents back in California to ask for help. She hated the idea, her dad after all had warned her of moving to Maine with Gerry. "He's a bum," he told her more than once. But now, being responsible for Rob, the situation was desperate.

Even though the full onslaught of winter hadn't settled in yet, it was still dark, cold and very quiet on the island as Annie walked to find a house with a phone. The streets were deserted. There was no noise, no cars, no one outside and not even a barking dog. Other than the wind going through the trees, it was dead. Annie had never heard it so quiet. It unnerved her.

A bit of panic set into Annie. She thought about going back to her house but what would she do there? Wait until the cold swallowed her and Rob? If she didn't have the baby, sure, she'd try to survive but she couldn't do that to Rob. He would freeze in that house with no heat. She needed to find a phone to call her folks and ask for some money, maybe even tickets to go back to California.

She made her way down a street in the center of the island when she finally saw street lights and heard dogs communicating. The sound of a back door opening and a voice yelling for the dogs to be quiet comforted her greatly. Finally there were houses with lights on and people moving around inside. Kids bicycles laying in front yards. What a glorious sight to behold. There was life after all! Praise the Good Lord!

Annie came across a house situated slightly above the road with a big front porch looking down on her. The house was well-lighted so it was quite easy to see inside from the darkened street where Annie stood. A

heavyset woman was moving around in what appeared to
be the kitchen.

Annie, desperate and cold, walked up the steps to
the front door and knocked. A roaring dog came running,
jumping at the door, growling and scratching at the
window with teeth glaring.

"Get down!" The woman yelled at the dog with a
very intimidating voice making Annie a bit nervous. Not
a lady anyone would want to mess with. She was big and
burly, her gray hair going in all directions, curly or just
unkempt Annie couldn't tell. The woman opened the
front door. "Oh, you're that young lady who just moved
to one of them summer homes up there, aintcha?" She
said with a deep Maine accent. Summer sounded like
someuh.

"Yes, ma'am," Annie replied. "But we have no
heat. And I have a baby. I don't know what to do."
Seemingly out of nowhere she started to cry.

"Come in, come in, lady. Warm yourself up. Sit
down at that table over there (ovah they-uh) and let me
get you some tea." Her kindness made Annie cry even
more. This big, gruff-looking woman was more motherly
than her own mother.

"Don't you worry, missy. We won't letcha
freeze." Then suddenly she yelled, "Jessica! Jessica!"
Which caused little Rob to jump.

"What mum?!?!" echoed a frustrated voice from
the other room where a TV was blaring.

"Get the missus here some tea."

"Mum! I'm trying to watch!" Was the exasperated response from the other room.

"Get her the tea or you'll be watchin' from the front porch!"

Annie intervened. "Oh it's okay, I don't need any tea."

"Oh yes you do… It's cold out there and look at your face. It's all red. You're freezing!"

Jessica came into the kitchen. A tall girl, probably no more than 16 and skinny as a nail.

"Thanks mum, right during the best part." Jessica sulked. Then, startled to see a stranger sitting with a baby at the kitchen table, she muttered, "oh, sorry," while looking at Annie sheepishly.

"No, not at all. That's okay. Thanks so much for getting me tea."

Jessica stood by the electric stove while her mom spoke to Annie.

"I'm Maggie by the way. This sunray here is Jessica," she said pointing to her daughter. "She is my 7th...and last! Ain't that right Jessie!" Maggie proceeded to laugh out loud. Snorting even.

"Yes mum, I'm your last," Jessica responded in a bored voice. "Never heard that before," she mumbled.

"Oh Jessie, you know I'm only kidding you. You are the best of my flock!" Maggie laughed harder this time, snorting even more.

She continued. "Yeah, ain't nothin like teenage girls, let me tell you, ummm...?" She looked at Annie confused. "Wait, what's your name?"

"Oh, right. Sorry. It's Anne but people call me Annie," Annie replied.

"Well great to meet you Annie. You don't look old enough to have teenage girls but let me tell ya, just you wait!" Maggie went back to laughing.

Jessica brought the tea over and set it down in front of Annie.

"Don't mind my mum, Ms. Annie," Jessica said. "She thinks she's a comedian. But notice the only one laughing is her." Then she walked back to the room where the TV was still blaring.

"Oh, that's not true, dear Jessica," Maggie called after her. "Your father *used* to laugh. I had him in stitches. And if I ever see his rear-end again, I'll put him in real stitches!" And Maggie erupted again.

Annie laughed which made Maggie laugh harder.

Jessica shouted from the TV room. "Mum, can you keep it down, for Heaven's sake! We don't need the whole island to hear you!"

Maggie waved her off, grinned and focused again on Annie. "She's got it good. She just don't know it yet." Then Maggie raised her voice for Jessica to hear. "Wait till she meets a scoundrel like her father. Then she'll realize how good she had it living here with her mum, ole Maggie!"

She looked directly at Annie, let out a deep sigh and asked, "so tell me about Miss Annie here. How'd you come to be on our little island and end up on my front porch?"

The comfort Annie felt in Maggie was immediate, as if Maggie was her surrogate mother, so much that she broke down again. All the frustration came out. The fear of raising a child with no help, the anger she had about being duped when she came to Maine and recognizing her husband simply wasn't capable. It all came out in an avalanche of tears.

Maggie just sat back and listened, allowing Annie to unload. Annie slowly began to regain her composure, feeling a huge weight being removed. She just needed someone to listen. Reality, unfortunately, was still bleak. She still had the problem of a freezing home with a husband who seemed to have checked out of his responsibilities.

"Jessica!" Maggie suddenly yelled out, startling Annie. "Come make our guest another cup of tea," Maggie ordered.

"Mom, I'm watching my show!" Jessica snapped back.

"You'll be lucky to have a TV to watch if you don't make that tea!"

Jessica shuffled back into the kitchen. "Mom, you know *you* can make it, right?" She asked sarcastically.

"Oh yes, my wonderful daughter but I wanted Miss Annie here to see that with a bit of patience, when her boy gets older, she can have a servant just like me!" Maggie started laughing and snorting again, slapping her knees.

Her laughter was contagious as Annie also was cracking up. She laughed so hard that the snot that had been built up from all her crying came out of her nose. When Maggie saw Annie's snot-infused laughing, she began to laugh even harder, causing her to have hiccups.

"She's a barrel of laughs, isn't she?" Jessica asked in a playful tone. "She's the funniest person in Maine, just ask her. She'll tell you."

And Maggie laughed even harder at Jessica's dig at her.

When things had died down and Jessica brought another cup of tea to Annie, Maggie said, "I'll be honest Annie, Jessie here is my pride and joy. She's everything to me. And sadly, she *knows* it!"

"Mum! You're embarrassing yourself!" Jessica yelled as she left the kitchen.

"She and I have been through a lot together. Maybe one day, if you stick around, I'll tell you the details. But for now, I want you to know things do get better. There's no guarantee of course, but they do. You've just been caught unprepared. Nothing wrong with that, especially when you're young. But things do get better." Maggie looked away, chuckled a bit and nodded her head as if remembering her own past.

"The issue is that you are not only responsible for yourself but also for your boy here." She stopped, paused and gave a quizzical look at the baby.

"Rob. Rob's his name," Annie interjected.

"Good to know, very good to know. What a fine looking boy. He's gonna be a lady-killer."

This whole time Rob sat peacefully on his mom's lap, barely uttering a sound. Just resting his head against her shoulder. His future self, though, wouldn't be this restful. Annie would never know that though.

Maggie continued. "Give your husband a couple days of living in that cold house of yours and he'll snap out of it. Why some summer person sold that to you knowing you'd be living there full-time, with a baby, is just evil if you ask me. But the deed is done. So, it's gotta be up to your husband to get his crap together and fix that place so you, and most importantly little Rob here, don't freeze this winter."

Maggie paused in thought, then said. "I have a crib in one of the bedrooms upstairs. You and Rob can stay here until that house of yours is habitable. If you've never been through a Maine winter, you don't know how bad it's gonna get. It's no place for a baby if the house ain't proper."

"I can't do that Maggie," Annie responded. "I just met you, and you've already been so kind."

Maggie scoffed. "Oh, this is not up for debate, Annie. No way I can let you go back to that freezing house. You think I could sleep knowing I sent a baby to a house that isn't ready for winter? Nope, not under my watch. So, you're staying here. Tomorrow you can go back to get some clothes but for tonight let's go and get you situated."

Anne began to cry again.

"Stop that! You've already had your crying fit," Maggie joked. "But really do stop that. You're going to make me cry if you keep it up and then Jessica will have no respect for me. Not that she does now anyway,"

And the laughter started again.

Winterizing

A loud commotion woke Gerry from sleeping off the previous night's binge. Gathered on the front lawn were about a half a dozen men with various tools looking like a full-on construction crew. In his hungover state, Gerry opened the front door to investigate but before he could utter a word one guy sarcastically yelled for all to hear, "well, well, well, Gerry's awake!"

Gerry looked at his watch and replied defensively, "it's only 7:15!"

"Gerry," the islander said, amused. "You have moved to an island made up of many lobsterman. 7:15 is our lunch hour!" The rest of the crew started laughing, almost mockingly.

Before Gerry could reply, the islander continued. "We're here to get your house fixed up for the winter so your wife and kid won't freeze to death. Now before you say or do something you'll regret, you really only have two choices in the matter. The first is you can help us so we can get the job done faster. Or you can try to stop us. But as you can see," he said while turning around and pointing to the men behind him. "You can't. So what do you say we get to work?"

While Gerry was cocky and arrogant, he wasn't stupid. He knew the house needed to be winterized and he knew he wasn't going to be able to get it done on his own. So, on his best behavior, he walked over to the islander who seemed to be the leader, stuck out his hand and said, "I can't tell you how much I appreciate this. Thank you all." A cheer went up among the men.

After a couple days of some serious sweat equity by many of the men on the island, the house became bearable for the cold winter that was to come.

"Should get you through a winter or two, but you're really gonna want to move into one of the year round houses down towards town," one of the men told Gerry. "These houses here just aren't built for year-round living."

"Just got to get some money saved," Gerry replied. A sentiment that was quickly forgotten.

Gerry's Gone

Gerry didn't last long on the island. As the winter months set in he went into Portland frequently. Sometimes he would stay the night in town, sometimes he'd be gone for days. Annie had no clue who he was with or where he was staying but whenever he came back to Peaks he acted weird, aloof, like he was up to no good and trying to hide something. Annie never asked where he was and Gerry never told her which was just as well because by then Annie realized her life with Rob would be without Gerry.

Gerry was just too immature to raise a family and it was best they went their separate ways. Gerry readily agreed when Annie proposed the idea to him. The divorce was amicable and rather inexpensive. No fight over custody. No property to split up either as they didn't own much.

While she was disappointed in the realization she had no future with Gerry, she had no regrets. Annie was happy. She was meeting great people on the island. People who cared for her and Rob. She also knew that if it weren't for Gerry, there'd be no Rob and Rob meant everything to her. Nothing was more important.

Annie was able to get by, but barely. Her parents helped her by paying the mortgage. But those payments always came with relentless "guidance" on how to live her life and "I told you so's" about moving to Maine with Gerry in the first place. That drove her crazy and she couldn't wait for the day when she would be able to get out from under their shadow.

She applied and received WIC benefits, AFDC, Medicaid, state of Maine heating assistance and any government program which would help put food on the table. Powdered milk and government cheese were staples at Annie's house. Between her parents and government aid, their basic essentials were met.

Annie always had a laugh when people looked contemptuously when she paid for groceries with her purple and orange Food Stamps. The idea of a welfare queen hadn't come into the vernacular yet, but some people gave the vibe they felt Annie was getting over on them. She'd think of her poorly insulated, very drafty summer cottage with an old furnace that probably spit out more fumes than actual heat and think "if this is getting over on people, well, so be it." Sure, there were some people taking advantage of the system, but for the vast majority on support, they certainly weren't living like kings.

Annie's gardening skills were improving and by the time the summer came she had more produce than she and Rob could possibly consume. She traded vegetables for various items she was in short supply of, butter, any kind of meat, fish, but also household items like light bulbs, sugar, toilet paper and even firewood, dried hardwood was a valuable commodity for dealing with the brutal Maine winters.

Annie would take Rob with her around the island to forage for blueberries which were bountiful. Together, they consumed some, canned some and traded the rest, all in preparation for winter. By the time the trees started turning the glorious colors of a New England fall, she felt she was as prepared as she could be for the upcoming blast of cold and wind. But she knew this was only temporary. Her house was a shelter, yes, but it was FAR from a home. No place to raise a young boy.

The house was remote, even for the island, because it was on the Northeast side where only summer vacationers had houses. There were no full-time residents who lived on that side of the island which frightened her when the dark days of winter returned. What if an emergency occurred, a NorEaster blasts through and smashes the roof? There would be no one to hear her cry for help. What if Gerry showed up? Who knew what kind of mood he'd be in.

Annie hoped to move into a house closer to where the year-rounders lived on the island. Where would she get the money though? Her parents already helped her buy this house even though they advised against it. Move off the island and get a job in Portland? If she did that she may as well just move back to California where the weather was better and jobs were plentiful. She liked being on the island; Loved it actually. It was exactly what she was hoping for when she and Gerry moved to Maine to begin with. A small community of people living more naturally than most people in the U.S.

And the people were so friendly too, always offering to lend a hand. The entire island loved Rob. They loved having young kids around and wished there were more.

"Not too many young-uns around here any more," people would say to Annie with their deep Maine accents when they saw her with Rob.

Initially, Anne couldn't understand some of the things they said. What confused her was that Mainers don't say "R" where it is supposed to be yet they sometimes put the "R'" where it isn't. "Mainer", for instance, becomes "Mainah". "Idea" somehow is pronounced "i-dear". The weirdest thing. Just another eccentricity of Maine that Annie loved.

"In ten years or so, there'll probably be no kids left on this island and no young adults either," Maggie once told Annie. "Kids today don't want to be here. They all move off the minute they get old enough. At that point it's just going to be us old folks and then some summer people. The community will be gone forever."

"I don't believe that at all, Maggie. This place is heavenly. It's like a step back in time, to a simpler, friendlier place."

"Uh-huh," Maggie replied. "Problem with that though, Annie, is people today don't want that. They want stuff. They want activity, excitement. They want the hustle and bustle of the city and not just Portland either. They want Boston, New York (pronounced New

Yahk). I don't blame 'em. But what happens to the island when all the younger folk are gone? Sad to think about."

"Oh Maggie, that's crazy. At least Rob and I will be here," Annie said in a most confident manner.

"Annie, I guarantee you, Rob'll be off this island the minute he can. There is nothing here for a young man."

"Maybe he'll be the start of a rebirth, Maggie, a resurgence of the island community!" Annie proclaimed proudly

Little did she know how right she and Maggie would *both* be.

GoodBye To Annie

After one more winter in her cottage Annie decided to sell her house to a summer resident from Massachusetts. The upgrades helped her pocket a decent profit. She was able to pay off the mortgage, making her parents happy, and sock a couple years' cash away into her savings account.

She didn't want to own another house, though, so she and Rob moved into a small rental across the street from Peaks Island School. While the place was too small to continue to raise chickens, Annie was able to garden. She was close enough to the beach that she had access to all the seaweed she needed to fertilize the soil and her garden boomed.

The next five years were the best of Annie's life. She was very active in the island community, particularly being a fierce advocate for an improvement in the boat service that took islanders back and forth to Portland.

She was also very involved in Rob's school. She would help out whenever they needed a parental volunteer. But more than that, when Rob came from school, Annie was right there, helping with homework, sharing with him her love of gardening and being in nature and just providing Rob the sense of security all children need.

Eventually, though, the money from the sale of the house ran out and Annie found herself having to get a job in town which meant the daily commute. Rob was now in middle school so he also had to commute into the city. He played sports and had friends in Portland so he would invariably get home well after dinner time. He and Annie were like two ships passing in the night and didn't see much of each other.

Rob was growing into a young man and the rebellious teenage years didn't pass him by. While Annie tried her best, it's hard for a single mom to raise a teenage boy. Dads are needed to drop the hammer when rebellion turns into outright revolution. But Rob's dad was long gone and it was just him and Annie in a battle of wills. Tensions frayed and stayed that way for years to come.

When Rob turned eighteen he immediately joined the Army and left the island, just like Maggie had predicted years earlier, and he never came back. Maybe it was good fortune that Rob left actually. He wasn't around to see the slow devastation that would take place in Annie's body from the skin cancer that developed and eventually killed her.

While they did communicate on occasion, Annie never let Rob know of her condition, even during her literal dying days. She didn't want to alarm him, he had a life to lead after all, with a wife and kids to worry about. Annie didn't want to add to his concerns. The only time

Rob came back to the island after he left was for Annie's funeral.

Part III

Internet Comes to Peaks Island

By the turn of the century, with a dwindling population and few children remaining, it appeared the year-round island community would be gone within a generation. To try to get younger people and families to move to the island The Peaks Island Association, Peaks' version of the Chamber of Commerce, received a grant of $50,000 from the city of Portland to market the island in newspapers and TV advertisements across Southern Maine. The reasoning was quite simple, if people didn't start moving to the island the city of Portland would have to take ownership of all the abandoned homes that were being left as the elderly population died off. The City leaders thought a $50,000 investment into an advertising campaign was small compared to whatever the City would have to spend later when the island was nearly vacant.

Unfortunately, the campaign was a dud and it seemed inevitable that Peaks would be nearly vacant of people in one generation, leaving empty houses and a decaying infrastructure. This would lead to big bucks having to be spent to raze the island or to provide cheap housing to indigent people, like the City did in the 1960s and 70s with disastrous results.

But fate won't be denied. A new hire in the Portland City Parks department, Ryan Glazier, made a suggestion at a Finance Committee meeting that changed Peaks Island forever. The Committee was meeting to discuss how much money, if any, to budget for maintenance of the decaying Peaks Island School athletic fields.

"I know we're about to end the campaign trying to get families to move to Peaks," Ryan nervously said to the committee. He was a new hire after all and the last thing Mainers wanted was for people from away, in this case Ryan had just relocated his family from Boston, to tell them how to run things. "I'm aware the marketing attempt didn't work well."

"We wasted a *lot* of money!" George Burgess, a grizzled man who'd been involved in city politics for decades and the Committee Chair, piped in. Burgess had different ideas on how to spend City money, mainly reinvigorating parts of Commercial Street which just so happened to be where his business was located.

Ryan nodded deferentially to him, inviting him to continue if he had more to say. Burgess just stared silently at him, looking bored. After an awkward silence, the Boston transplant continued.

"Has anyone thought about advertising via social media to families in Boston? I know there are families who are fed up with the costs of living and crime down there. And I know they'd love to leave if they could. My own family did that just last year as a matter of fact."

Ryan explained how young families weren't reading newspapers or watching local news anymore. So they didn't even see the advertisements of the Peaks Association. The only people who had seen the advertisements promoting Peaks were older people who still read newspapers and already lived in Maine. If they wanted to move to Peaks, they already would have done so. The campaign needed to market to families in bigger, more expensive cities that wanted to move out for a quieter, safer life, which Peaks could provide at a much lower cost of living.

"To make this successful people are going to have to be able to find work though," Ryan continued. "It's tough for a family to leave a big city to come up to Peaks if they don't have a job lined up. This is where it gets exciting, however. Remote working is becoming all the rage. People can work at their current jobs yet live on Peaks but only if we get high speed internet out there. So I'd like to suggest the City of Portland invest to get the island wired."

George Burgess interrupted. "I noticed *you* didn't move to Peaks when you moved up here, Mr. Glazier. And yet you're telling us to spend all this money because other people will? Seems fanciful to me." Burgess then crossed his arms and sat back in his chair indicating the debate was over.

Ryan was quick on his feet though. "Mr. Burgess, my family *would* have moved to Peaks if there was high-speed internet. We actually toured the island and loved it. But both my wife and I need high-speed internet access to get our jobs done. Without it we couldn't move there."

Another Committee member jumped in before Burgess could respond. "I think that's a great idea! My own son lives in Portland but works for a company out of Boston. He talks about how much he loves it on Peaks. He goes there a lot actually. I propose Portland invest to provide high speed internet access to the island. After all, we have it here in town already. It's a matter of equity." Equity, of course, being the trendy word of the early 21st century that no liberal could be seen as being against. The fact that Portland was run by liberals sealed the proposal.

Another proposal was added to give the campaign an even bigger boost; The City of Portland would offer a $20,000 incentive for any family to relocate. That $20,000 could be used for anything as long as the family stayed on the island for at least 3 years.

After a few minutes of debate and over the fierce objections of George Burgess, the Finance Committee voted to spend more money on the Peaks campaign. Burgess, who was red-faced when the vote was announced, shot Ryan an icy look and stormed out of the meeting.

It took a few months for the new campaign to gain traction but word got out. Suddenly, people from all over the country were inquiring about moving to Peaks. In less than a year's time, the City of Portland had ten times the number of people contacting them about relocating than they had budgeted for. At that point, the City discontinued the campaign but that didn't stop people from looking at Peaks Island to relocate. The addition of high speed internet changed everything.

The one bottleneck that remained was the lack of reliable boat transportation to Peaks. Given so much interest had been generated by the marketing plan, they couldn't let the whole thing fail due to bad boat service. The City of Portland voted to issue bonds to create the Casco Bay Authority to make sure the boats ran efficiently, safely and reliably.

Whereas most government "investments" are nothing more than spending programs geared towards enriching politicians' campaign donors, these investments actually paid off. People began moving to the island, property values began to increase as well as tax revenues, a huge help for Portland's budget.

The number of full time residents on the island increased by 250%. Even George Burgess, who was so adamantly against the campaign, benefited. The increase in traffic to Peaks meant an increase in traffic along Commercial Street in Portland where the wharfs were, which was where George Burgess had his business interests. In a few years time that location became some of the most expensive real estate in the entire state of Maine. Luxury condo developments went up with lots of artisan shops within walking distance of the boats. Burgess, it turned out, benefitted more than anyone from the Peaks Island renaissance.

Gentrification

It didn't take long before it became apparent the Peaks Island Plan had gone off script though. The first to relocate to Peaks were childless professionals from Boston, lured by low crime, cheap property values and the new ability to work from home. They bought the older homes overlooking the water and immediately began tearing them down in order to replace them with monstrosities that didn't fit in with the rest of the island.

Wasn't long before the island had become overrun by tear-downs, driving up the prices of the rest of the homes on the island. Higher property values sound good in theory but until one sells their home, higher property values simply means higher property tax. Increased taxes were not an expense many of the long term residents of Peaks could easily afford especially those on fixed incomes.

The old-timers lobbied for discounted property tax rates for residents on a fixed income but the City denied their request. The city leaders needed tax money and the revenue boost Peaks was now providing was pure gold to them. The residents could always sell at a nice premium to what they paid and take the money and run.

The question of "run to where, exactly?" was never answered. Or "what if I don't want to leave?" Those concerns mattered not when it came to the almighty tax dollar the wealthy new-comers were bringing in.

As far as those who complained about the island community being changed, they were met with the standard "embrace change or get out of the way." Who cared if it changed the community anyway? The community was dying before and now it is being reinvigorated!

When anyone brought up that the intent of the Peaks Island Plan was to bring families back to the island, not the wealthy with no kids, the rebuttal was "so what if there was no one raising families on the island anymore. The state of Maine had the oldest population in the nation. Schools were being closed or consolidated state-wide. That this was happening on Peaks too should be of no surprise to anyone. Oh, by the way, these newcomers, these wealthy empty-nesters, were just like the established islanders anyway; They wanted a safe, peaceful place to call home."

Furthermore, as it was repeatedly mentioned, not only did the newcomers pay more in taxes than the older residents, they actually cost the city less too. The older folks, many of whom were heavily reliant on government services, were a big cost to the Portland taxpayers. For the City of Portland the gentrification on Peaks Island was a very welcome turn of events they hadn't expected.

Down With Compost!

Unfortunately, the newcomers didn't stop at just changing the housing stock on the island, they took over the Island Association as well and began to issue regulations.
No more front yard gardens. No more compost piles at personal residences. Yards had to be maintained. Boats could not be anchored just anywhere, they had to be placed in defined areas. No more taking down trees without an arborist's approval. Foraging for blueberries on public land was illegal. The last thing the new residents wanted was locals walking around the island picking blueberries for personal consumption. Blueberries were a public good after all. Better to have the blueberries rot and go to waste than someone actually getting more than their "fair share".

When grandkids came to visit they were forbidden from using ATVs or golf carts on public land or roads. It was also prohibited for anyone to jump off the wharf into the swells of the car ferry as had been a tradition among island kids for generations. Can't have people getting hurt and suing the city. If you smoked, you couldn't smoke on the beach and definitely no more open containers!

Some of the older residents didn't like the new regulations.

"I've always had a compost pit. What's wrong with composting?" One old-timer asked at a council meeting.

"We absolutely *love* compositing, it's organic after all," was the patronizing response from the town council. "We just don't think people should be doing it in our neighborhoods. It has a smell and brings lots of flies and other critters too, some of which could be harmful and impact the quality of life of your neighbors. So, we ask you to compost in the community garden that we've established at the Ballfield."

"But I compost everything, including table scraps. I can't just go up to the ballfield after every meal and throw it on the compost pile."

"No, we wouldn't expect you to do that. And while we know it's an inconvenience for the *few* who actually still want to compost at their homes, we suggest just throwing your scraps into a compostable trash bag and taking it up to the community garden every now and again."

The logic, of course, was nonsensical but it didn't matter to the newcomers. They wanted everything on their idyllic island life to look clean and proper. Rain catchment barrels in the front of one's house were prohibited. No more motorcycles parked in front of homes. No more cars being worked on in the yards of residents either. It had to be done in a garage where no one could see it. Of course, most islanders didn't have garages but that was not a concern of the new leadership who wanted their very own Martha's Vineyard in Maine, a haven for the exclusive.

The list of things one could not do in polite society got longer every time the Island Association met.

Don't just throw your trash in the trash can, you need to recycle it in one of four different recycling bins. The town will send recycling crews around to inspect your trash. They're not there to issue tickets of course (not yet), but they'll help recycling efforts by pointing out how you could do better. It's for the good of the environment, after all, and everyone benefits from being green.

You wanted to build a deck on your home? Need Council approval for that and your plans needed to be very specific to be appealing to a passer-by.

The Council advocated a clean air tax for any resident who drove a non-electric vehicle. They advocated a carbon tax for anyone heating their home with fossil fuels. They incorporated a fee for any resident whose electricity usage was more than a fixed amount. Given there were few kids left on the island this wouldn't be a burden to most. If you had kids though and your electricity bill was higher than what the Council considered it should be...well. To those who complained they were met with the standard rebuttal, "Well, houses *are* selling at a premium so there was nothing to stop one from selling and moving off the island with a sizable profit." Get the hint?

The newcomers, many of whom were vegan, were especially eager to reduce, if not outright stop, lobstering which had been a staple of Peaks Island for centuries.

The recent arrivals looked at these regulations quite favorably. They could afford higher fees, taxes and increased restrictions. They were also able to pay for better insulation in their homes. Thicker windows. Many invested in grid-tied solar arrays to provide some of their electricity and they were able to receive subsidized utility bills as well. But for the traditional, older residents, with limited resources, living on the island became much more expensive. They couldn't afford to invest in roof-top solar, for instance. So, not only did they have to pay increased utility bills because of their fossil fuel use but they were also subsidizing the utility bills of the wealthy who installed solar panels! A reverse-Robinhood tax scheme if there ever was one.

Since the island was part of the City of Portland many of the local ordinances had to be approved by the Portland City Council. Approvals were pretty easy to come by though.The newcomers were a very left-wing, politically-active bunch with money to make their voices heard and usually what they wanted they got.

To keep the island quaint, or exclusive, truth be told, no further development was allowed other than a tear down or an add-on to an existing home. You had a piece of land you wanted to put a house on? Not going to happen under the new regulatory scheme. Housing supply was now greatly limited meaning any house that went for sale was subject to an immediate bidding war, increasing the sales price. No middle or lower income family was able to afford a house on the island anymore. It was a win-win for the newcomers; Keep the lower income people from moving in and drive up costs for those the old-timers, essentially forcing them to sell and move off. Exclusivity was the order of the day for the newcomers to Peaks Island.

5th Maine

There was a spark of resistance among locals when they found out the 5th Maine Regiment historical museum had been sold to a corporate lawyer from Cambridge, Massachusetts. The museum was located in an old Victorian overlooking the ocean on Back Shore; A premium location on the island.

The museum trustees said they couldn't afford to keep operating it as foot traffic had declined 80% and the cost of operations greatly exceeded the small amount of revenue generated. So the only option was to sell, and so they did, for a song. At the next Island council meeting when the ownership change was announced it was not well received.

"You guys never said to anyone on the island you were in trouble financially," one of the residents stated to the trustees.

"We've known for a while that we were going to have to do this," was the response. "We just wanted to keep it quiet and not bring any bad press to the island, especially with the Peaks Plan going."

"Odd how you had a buyer already lined up even though you were trying to keep it quiet," another resident said. "How did he even know about this if folks on the island were kept in the dark?" Many of the other residents in attendance nodded in agreement.

"Well, our books are available online for anyone to see. All non-profits are. Mr. Weaver, the gentleman who made the purchase, just happened to do the research. He recognized our plight and contacted us with an offer. We didn't feel it appropriate to bring attention to the public that the 5th Maine was failing. The media would then naturally ask why it was failing and who knows what kind of bad publicity that would bring to the island. We wanted to avoid all that. Remember what happened the last time we had a deluge of media inquiries."

The islanders had to agree that this made sense. The last thing they needed was bad press. A generation earlier Peaks had been known as Welfare Island and many articles were written disparaging the islanders. It took a long time to overcome that stigma. So the pushback was quickly dropped and the 5th Maine changed hands.

Unbeknownst to the locals, was that Mr. Weaver specialized in turning old, strategically located buildings into very high-end condos. He was planning on converting the 5th Maine into six waterfront luxury units. Given the additional property tax revenue the condos would generate, he was confident he could get the blessing of the City of Portland Planning Commission to approve his plan even if the locals put up a stink.

By the time the islanders were keen to the plan of further gentrification it was too late to do anything. Approval had been granted, permits were placed and the machine of "progress" rolled on, rolling over whatever was in its path, in this case, local islanders and their quaint community.

Part IV

Rob Returns to Peaks

It was a bright mid-October day when Rob McKenzie went back to Peaks Island for the first time in decades. As the boat approached the island it seemed surreal. Has it really been over *thirty* years? In a lot of ways, it felt like he never left. The smell was exactly like it was when he was a kid. Over the years when he'd come across certain scents Rob would do a double take, as for a quick moment his mind would be taken back to his days in Maine.

It's amazing that a *smell* can stay with you throughout your life and bring back memories from days long past. A smell is just a temporary sensation which occurs hundreds if not thousands of times a day and yet whenever Rob got a sniff of a horse barn, for instance, it made him think of the Fryeburg Fair, Maine's largest county fair that is held each fall. He'd only attended that fair one time and yet every time he smelled a horse barn he would think of it.

Why do smells bring back memories of the past? Why did the smell of a fresh rain falling on an asphalt street that had been baking in the summer sun remind Rob of Peaks Island? Was it because those were the first instances of these various smells in Rob's life and thus they were forever tattooed in his memory?

The mysteries of the human mind are breathtaking to think about. But the human mind could also play tricks, no? Is that what happened to Marcus to cause him to commit suicide? Did his mind lead him to such a dark place he could never escape from? This was what worried Rob. Could his mind lead him to do something as dramatic? The idea definitely scared him.

God Paints Peaks Island

The fall colors dominated the landscape of the island just as beautifully as ever. Rob could stare at the cornucopia forever in amazement. Talk about eye candy. The spastic colors were as sure a sign of a Creator as anything Rob could imagine. Every year, the exact trees that witnessed generations of kids grow up on Peaks Island would offer their testimony by producing the most beautiful color combinations no man could create.

After living in the Arizona desert for so many years, surrounded by brown, Rob simply couldn't take his eyes off these amazing specimens. A tiny seed that germinated decades before now stood forty, fifty feet off the ground. The energy density in all that wood, the ability to defeat the so-called laws of gravity by forcing water dozens of feet above the ground, the mulch of the fallen leaves adding nutrients to soil that was being decimated by mankind's monoculture farming practices, a home for other creatures of God, the trees are literal life. Rob just stared in awe. "How have I abandoned you?" he asked himself and he could almost hear the trees whisper "welcome back, old friend."

While the landscape and smells of the island were just as Rob remembered everything else had changed. The very landing where the boat docked was completely different. The old, crumbling, wooden wharf was replaced by one of all steel. The car ferry dock, which was hardly <u>used</u> before, now was prominent, jutting out into the bay awaiting the arrival of boats filled with the vehicles. When Rob grew up he couldn't remember if the car ferry even ran more than once or twice a day as very few islanders had cars to justify it. Now it seemed to be the primary mode of transportation to get people on and off the island. In fact, it was the car ferry that brought Rob to Peaks, even though he had no vehicle.

He got off the boat and walked up the cobblestone street past a line of idling cars waiting to be taken to Portland. One-by-one the drivers waited in their cars, windows up, looking stoically at their phones. None could be bothered to even look at Rob as he walked by, never mind offer a wave.

In the old days, bundled-up Islanders gathered together on the wharf waiting for the boat while the cold winds ripped through them. There was something to be said about everyone fighting the cold together, freezing in unison. Rich and poor, young and old, all suffering in the same way. It created a sense of community.

Sitting in your car with the heat on removed from the rest of the world seemed endemic to the current state of the country. Everyone in their own world, with no involvement whatsoever with others around them. Was it any surprise that narcissism was growing rapidly in America?

As Rob continued up the hill towards Island Avenue he was amazed at how many shops there were now. They were all closed currently because the tourist season was over but come May, they'd be hopping, booming with business. Summer times were always busy on Peaks even when Rob was a kid but now it must be pure chaos. After all, while the physical size of the island was the exact same as it had been for thousands of years, the number of stores now lining the streets meant there must be a heck of a lot more people in the summer.

Every house Rob walked by had a golf cart parked out front. Rob smiled at this because when he was growing up hardly anyone had a car, never mind a golf cart. Back then people just walked everywhere. Now most residents had a car *and* a golf cart. Did anyone walk anymore?

The Cashier

Peaks Island still had just one grocery store. No longer called Feeney's, now it was Hanover Market and its sign out front read "Organic Specialists".

Rob went in to get a snack. The place definitely had changed. It was a modern day store now with an urban, hipster vibe, earth tone colors and progressive rock music in the background. It was like Brooklyn-on-Peaks to include the expensive prices too. Yet, it was hopping with customers.

"Lots of tourists today, eh?" Rob asked the 50-ish clerk with circular, horn-rimmed glasses, facial hair and sleeve tattoos ringing him up.

"Oh, I don't think so," he responded. "Tourist season is well behind us."

"Wow," Rob said. "Lots of locals shopping then, huh?"

"Not really," the clerk answered. "These folks are just picking up their Amazon and UPS packages. You're not from here, are you?"

"Well, I grew up here. Been decades since I've been back though," Rob replied.

"Cool!" The cashier said very pleasantly. "Where are you visiting from?"

"Phoenix, as a matter of fact," Rob responded.

"Well, welcome back! The island is definitely different from what you remember, I imagine."

"Indeed, golf carts are everywhere!" Rob said with a chuckle. "No one had a golf cart when I was growing up." Rob paused then asked, "how long have you been here?"

The clerk snickered. "A long time. Longer than most, actually."

"You went to school here?" Rob asked.

"Oh, no, nothing like that. I'm from Boston and we used to summer here. I've always loved the island. The people here back then though, well, they didn't do it for me. A bit set in their ways." Then he remembered that Rob said he used to live here. "No offense, of course."

"Oh, none taken," Rob replied. "I know what you mean, actually. That's one of the reasons I moved off."

Now thinking Rob was a fellow-traveler, the clerk continued, "it's when we got high speed internet that changed everything. A whole new group of people moved here. More tolerant, more open minded. My wife was already working from home in Boston and she also loved the island, so when high-speed internet became available we just up and moved."

Rob wondered why this guy thought the previous island folks weren't tolerant and open-minded. It was always a hippie place, known for being eclectic and eccentric. There were openly gay people on the island during a time when it was still basically a crime to be gay. This guy obviously didn't know the history of Peaks.

"Well, you lived here," the clerk continued. "You know how it was with a lot of the older folks. Some of them were liberal but still reactionary. Forcing their gender preferences on children and, well, you know, all that right-wing crap. My wife and I certainly didn't want to live in a place where our tax dollars supported that in the schools. If we had kids we'd definitely raise them so that it's okay to be gender fluid." The clerk stated proudly.

"There are a lot of attorneys here now," he continued. "Lots of corporate counsel types, like my wife. She works for a firm in Boston, goes down once a month. But everything else she does from home. We don't even need to commute to Portland!"

"Is the school still here?" Rob asked.

"For now it is. It's getting tough to keep it open though. Just not enough kids."

"Oh man, that's too bad." Rob couldn't imagine what the elementary school kids would do if Peaks Island School was closed down. 2nd graders commuting to Portland did not sound like a good thing at all.

"Well, we are very conscious about the environment here. And take our footprint seriously. Children are a burden to the planet. That we know," the clerk stated matter-of-factly.

"Oh, I hear you…" Rob muttered. Oh boy, another kool aid drinker. People are the cause of environmental degradation. Thus by having kids you're contributing to the destruction of the earth.

"Most people here don't have kids," the clerk said. "So, it's hard to see how the school will remain open in a few years. That's actually a good thing, believe it or not. Like I said, we have to do our part to protect the environment."

Rob didn't want to get into a debate about children causing climate change so he changed the topic.

"Do you guys stay busy during the winter?" he asked. During the winter, when the tourists were gone, the island had a fifth of the people it did in the summer.

"We do. But not with the groceries so much. We've become a UPS affiliate, pick up and ship out for Amazon too. That's what keeps us busy and why most of these people are here right now. They're all here for their packages. Notice there is no one in line behind you," he said with a laugh.

"We do sell *some* groceries, but certainly not enough to keep us in business. I imagine I won't be ringing anyone up for groceries in a year or two. Everything will be automated. And then I'll have to figure out something else to do. Thankfully, my wife has her job. I just work here to talk to folks."

"Really?" Rob said. "Your sign says 'Organic Specialists'. I would have thought you'd be selling lots of organic produce if nothing else."

"Oh we used to. We sold a ton of organic produce. We got our products from Aroostook County, delivered once a week. And, let me tell you, that produce was not cheap. But, if you wanted organic and lived on the island, pretty much we were your only option.

"The internet changed all that. Now you can buy organic that is grown and shipped from California cheaper than what you'd pay for Maine-grown products. Organic buyers are still price conscious so the cheapest price wins, as long as the product is stamped organic by the USDA.

"At one time we even had some folks growing organic crops for us right here on Peaks. To be profitable, though, they had to charge higher prices than what was coming in from California where the labor is cheap. People here still bought from the Californians as opposed to paying a bit more for local, literally grown on the very island itself, by people they knew! Things got pretty intense around here for a bit. Ultimately the local growers got fed up and left. They pointed out all the pollution and CO2 that was spewed by shipping goods cross-continent, but turns out price matters most, even for the supposedly environmentally-conscious."

"Oh, man, I'm sorry to hear that," Rob replied. "Can't say I'm surprised though, organic products do cost a lot."

"Yeah, but when you have cheap labor, like what they have all over California, you can undercut prices and ultimately drive your competitors out of business." Rob sensed the frustration, like maybe the organic, "green" life wasn't all it was shown to be?

"My friends were the growers," the clerk continued in a rather hostile way. "*I* was the one who encouraged them to move here because the price of produce from Aroostook County was so high. I told them there was a huge market for their products, especially as wealthier, more health-conscious people moved to the island. But the locals just wouldn't support them if it cost a few cents more!"

The clerk paused, seeming embarrassed after becoming aware he was at work and getting riled up. The pause gave Rob a chance to gather his items to head for the exit.

"Well it was good talking to you," Rob said as he started for the door.

"You too," the clerk relaxed again. "Where are you off to by the way?"

"I'm going to see Rachel DuBois. We actually went to school together here and I haven't seen her since. Been decades."

The cashier had a rather surprised look. "Ahh, Ms. DuBois," he uttered while nodding his head and almost grimacing.

Rob noticed his reaction and asked, "What? Is there something I should know?"

"Oh, no, no, no. I don't want to give you the wrong impression. Ms. Dubois is fine," he said, a bit sarcastically Rob thought. "Eccentric, but harmless."

"Oh, okay… well thanks again," Rob said and walked out the door. That was weird. Rachel is "harmless"? What's that supposed to mean? Is there something wrong or odd about seeing Rachel? What he had gotten himself into?

Rachel's House

Rob walked the half mile or so to Rachel's house which was on the south end of the island. When he was growing up the south end always seemed darker, almost creepy, due to the large canopy of trees. The change from sunshine on the rest of the island to shade here felt ominous, similar to going to a day-time movie; the lobby is bright and active and then you go into a dark, quiet theater, the mood changes dramatically.

He hardly ever came out here other than when he had his paper route. How he hated having to deliver papers when it got dark out here. Other than porch lights from people's houses there was no light once the sun went down. There weren't even street lamps. Collecting the money was even worse. He'd have to knock on the doors of the customers and ask for the money for their newspaper subscriptions. There was this feeling that over here something dark was going on behind those doors. So *of course* it was on this side of the island where Rachel lived. If Rachel was eccentric, as the cashier implied, where else would she live?

Rob found Rachel's cottage hidden in the dark shade of large maples well back from the road, a dirt path leading to the front door. A limited amount of the October sunshine sneaked through the trees, warning him the sun was finishing up its day and soon it would get very dark. Nothing creepy about this whole situation, no, nothing at all.

Rachel Welcomes Rob

Rob was apprehensive as he approached Rachel's house. What am I doing here? He wondered. Last chance to turn away and go back to Phoenix. But then, almost against his very will, his fist knocked on the door.

Immediately Rachel opened. So fast, in fact, that it startled Rob and he jumped back.

"Hey Rob!" She nearly shouted in a most welcoming way. "Didn't mean to scare you there. It's just so great to see you. Been way too long!" She gave Rob a hearty hug.

She was a smallish lady but appeared in good shape. Not skinny but slender. Like someone who isn't afraid to eat a big meal but does enough physical activity to keep the excess off.

"Wow Rachel," Rob said as they separated. "I wasn't expecting such a kind welcome. Thanks so much."

"Well, I love it when friends from the old days show up. And I can't tell you how excited I am to see you. Come on in. Mi Casa es Su Casa, as they say."

Rachel's house was typical for a Maine summer cottage, about 900 sq. feet or so. Downstairs consisted of a kitchen, smallish front room and dining room. Upstairs was just two small bedrooms and one bathroom. Nothing much, but certainly enough for one or two people to live.

"This place winterized Rachel?" Rob asked, remembering the cold he and his mom suffered through while living in the cottage he grew up in.

"It is now!" Rachel exclaimed. "Wasn't when I moved here and that first winter was a bear. Old insulation. Old furnace, single pane windows. There was a sweet lady who used to live here. I don't know how she dealt with the cold. But she did. I guess she just got used to it. But I was *miserable* that first year. So my first order of business was to get heavy insulation and upgrade the electrical and furnace. Cost me an arm and a leg. So, this place is basically a money pit. But now that I'm settled, I will never leave. I'm stuck here forever!" She said laughing.

Rachel invited Rob to sit down on one of the front room chairs.

"Get you a drink, beer, coffee, tea?"

"Haven't had a beer in 25 years but I'll take some water if you don't mind."

"Not at all," Rachel said and went into the kitchen to grab the water for Rob.

"What brought you back here, Rachel?" Rob called out while she was in the kitchen.

"A number of things," she said. "Hold on just a second and I'll tell you about it." Then she reappeared with a cup of ice water for Rob and tea for herself and sat down on the chair across from him.

"25 years without drinking, eh? There's a story to that obviously," Rachel said. Then she was quiet, inviting Rob to tell his story.

Rob took a drink of the water and immediately remembered how cold and fresh the Maine water was straight from the faucet.

"Oh man, is there anything better than Maine water?" Rob asked. "I forgot how good this tastes."

"Straight from Sebago lake," Rachel replied with a smile.

Rob nodded, took another drink, set his cup down and sat back in his chair, recognizing that Rachel was wanting him to share his history.

"Don't we all have a story," he said, somewhat sheepishly. "Well for me it was just being an angry young man. Don't really know why. But I always carried this chip on my shoulder. Throw in some alcohol and bad things happen.

"Got into a lot of fights. Hurt some people and got hurt myself too. Could never keep a relationship. Just wandering aimlessly, not really good at anything, not interested in anything either other than the one thing I liked to do and was very good at, drinking beer. Drinking allowed me to be someone I am not, outgoing and fun… at least that's what I thought."

Rob paused, allowing Rachel to speak. She stayed silent so Rob kept going.

"Then I woke up one morning with blood on my shirt. At first I thought I got a bloody nose while I was sleeping. But then I remembered what happened the night before; I beat the hell out of a good friend for no reason other than I was pissed at the world and he must have said something that triggered me. I felt guilty as hell and just laid there in bed, not believing that this happened, *again*. Another fight. What the hell was wrong with me? I kept asking myself.

I just needed someone to talk to. I grabbed the phone to call my girlfriend, Sandy, but then I remembered she had dumped me weeks before. All my friends were drinking buddies so I didn't want to talk to them. I basically had no one to talk to. It was depressing."

"Well, obviously things got better because you ended up marrying Sandy and you're still married, no?" Sandy asked.

"Yeah, pretty weird how life works," Rob said. "Wait, how'd you know I was married to Sandy?"

Rachel grinned and said, "Well, in anticipation of you coming, I was snooping a bit on social media."

Rob shrugged and continued. "Well, it was in college when I met Sandy. She was way too good for me. I was an immature punk, trying too hard to impress people. The same story for many young men, feeling a need to prove to the world they're tough as nails when in reality they're emotional wrecks. But Sandy eventually tired of my immaturity and dumped me. I really couldn't blame her as I was just drinking too much.

Then, one day out of nowhere, Sandy called. It'd been at least a month since we last talked. I couldn't believe it, hard for me to believe it still. When I saw it was her on the caller ID, I jumped at the phone and answered as fast as I could, worried she may have made a mistake in calling me and would hang up. Instead, she awkwardly asked if I could give her a ride.

She was moving to Boston for graduate school and had rented a U-Haul to move her stuff. Apparently her brother had forgotten he was supposed to take her and the place was going to close in an hour. If she didn't get her truck by close of business she'd lose her reservation. So in desperation, she contacted me as she couldn't get hold of anyone else.

When I drove her to the U-Haul place I could tell she was not happy having to rely on me. I gave her space and we just had a casual conversation. Now, this was in the days before cell phones, back when your phone number changed every time you moved. So when I dropped her off I knew that if I didn't get her new phone number I'd probably never talk to her again. As she was getting out of the car I told myself I can't just let her go like this and I asked for her new number in Boston.

I knew she didn't want to give it to me as she wanted to start a new life up there. But she paused for a moment, sighed, and then said, "do you have a pen and paper?" Luckily enough, I did.

That night I called her to make sure she arrived okay. She actually seemed happy that I called and we chatted a bit. I told myself right then and there that regardless of what happened with her, I'd never drink again. And I haven't, 25 years now, which I'm extremely proud of."

"You should be, Rob," Rachel interjected.

"But for the Grace of God," Rob said softly and then continued. "A year later, I was finishing up my degree and had no clue what I was going to do with the rest of my life. One lonely Saturday morning I was just sitting around the house I was renting. Now, remember, I had quit drinking by this time so all the friends I had were out of my life now and I didn't really have any new friends. I was pretty lonely.

I had the radio on for some background noise when that song "Iris" from The Goo-Goo Dolls came on. Not really my kind of music but man did that song hit me hard. I just paused in place, listening and really beating myself up for blowing it with Sandy. I can't remember if I had tears or not but I do remember I never felt that sad in my life, just in a fog, not suicidal or anything, I've never had that as an issue. But just empty. Such a horrible feeling.

Then, out of nowhere, the phone rang. It was Sandy, again! Almost as if it were Divine Intervention. There really is no other way to look at it. She was calling to invite me to visit her in Boston. We had exchanged a few emails since she moved but it was all formal stuff, nothing deep or anything. I thought she had moved on. But here she was calling me. And the rest is history. We've been married over 20 years.

Like most Americans, though, now we are stuck on the typical American gerbil wheel of living to work. It's kind of depressing actually." Rob paused a bit. Then muttered, "at least we're getting by, could be worse."

But they weren't really getting by. Things were falling apart on the home front which Rob neglected to share with Rachel. But he didn't have to tell her. She knew.

Rachel's Story

"Allright, I've told you my story, now let's hear yours. How did you end up back on the island?" Rob asked.

Rachel paused for a few moments, seeming to gather her thoughts. Then said, "I don't know how much you remember of me from when we were in school together but I was an angel student. I was indeed," she laughed.

"In school, I learned that being a teacher's pet gave you privileges the other kids didn't get, like good grades you didn't really deserve. Oh now don't get me wrong, I did work hard but I would always get the benefit of the doubt if there was a questionable grade."

"That's right!" Rob jumped in. "I do remember you! Always sitting in the first row. Always reminding the teacher to give homework and basically telling on anyone when they weren't doing what they were told!"

"Yup, that was me. Can't say I'm proud of it. But there you go. I'm not one to blame my parents, but they were pretty adamant of doing *whatever* it took to get good grades. Good grades meant a good life in their eyes. Sadly, in high school being a teacher's pet takes a new approach...if you know what I'm saying."

Rob nodded. He had a pretty good idea.

"Well, little did I realize when I was in high school that I got lucky in not getting knocked up. So I went to college and tried the same tricks with my male professors there. It's easy actually. Men really don't know how to say no and can be exploited very easily. I got the grades my parents needed to see to continue to pay for my lifestyle, which by then was partying all the time, lots of drinking and occasionally getting high.

I ended up getting pregnant by one of my professors, unfortunately. Now, while my family wasn't very religious growing up, we *were* Catholic. So being pregnant and not married isn't an easy thing, even for a C&E Catholic girl. "

Rob was confused. "What's C&E?"

"Oh, that means Christmas and Easter, C&E. Catholicism is filled with those kinds of adherents that just show up on Christmas and Easter. It's slowly becoming just E Catholics as many don't even go to service on Christmas anymore.

"Interesting," Rob said. "Never knew that."

"Well, while my professor tried to make it seem like an abortion is an easy thing, I had cold feet. I was *Catholic* after all. Because I was hesitant he began accusing me of all kinds of things, like tricking him to deliberately get pregnant. Mind you, I was just barely 19 years old and this is a guy in his 40's, way more experienced in the ways of the world and here he was trying to guilt me into getting an abortion.

When it appeared I wouldn't back down and would have the baby, he changed tact, saying he'd leave his wife for me if I only had an abortion. He made it seem we'd be together. He said he wasn't ready for more children as he already had two. But we could start a life together and he painted this whole romantic picture.

I fell for it and against my better instincts, I had the abortion. I went alone to the clinic and it was horrible, no matter what anyone says. It was devastating. When I left, I went straight to his office thinking he'd be there to console me and at least tell me I made the right decision. Oh, how naïve I was."

She grimaced, closed her eyes and threw her head back, obviously the experience was still painful. After a long, drawn out deep breath she continued.

"I walked into his office and he's sitting there at his desk, his head down, looks like he's grading papers. He hardly acknowledges me when I go in. So I tell him about what I just did and he barely moves his head, just looks at me over his reading glasses and mutters, "good, but I have work to do." Those were his exact words and the look he gave me was one of pure disgust. Like how dare I darken his door. I couldn't believe it.

'I thought you'd be happy,' I said, completely shocked by his callousness. 'Now we can be together. Just like you said.'

'You know I'm married and have kids, right?' He said.

I just stood there, dazed. Darkness began to engulf me, like I was being pulled deep into a black water. 'You said if I didn't have the baby…' and I said no more. He just stared at me, over his glasses, not even the courtesy to lift up his head to look at me. For some reason his look of pure disdain got to me, the darkness overtook me. I became so light-headed it felt as if my feet were no longer on the ground. I knew I was going to faint and tried to steady myself but I couldn't. The last thing I saw before I hit the ground was his face and for a fleeting moment it turned pure evil, like the Devil himself staring at me, except he no longer looked at me in disdain, now he was laughing, mocking me. He tricked me.

Next thing I remember, I was laying in a bed in the nurse's office wondering what happened. The nurse saw my eyes open and said, "you're going to be fine Rachel. You just fainted. It is allergy season after all." But I still remembered the professor's face, the demon that was behind it and how much that terrified me.

"After that, he denied ever knowing me other than me being a student in his class. I really didn't have any proof of our relationship either so I became despondent and began to lose it. I couldn't let him get away with this. I went to his wife. Let's just put it this way; I looked like a foolish kid with a crush on a professor who had rejected me. Happens all the time, right? Well, ultimately I got kicked out of school for lodging a "false accusation".

I was absolutely devastated. My life was thrown upside down. I could tell I was losing it, going crazy. I thought about contacting my parents but I couldn't. I didn't want them to know. They'd be so disappointed. The only way I could keep my sanity was to get high and thus began my long descent into drugs and just scraping by, day after day, year after year. I had normal jobs at first. But eventually I couldn't hold any down as my need to use grew. I even took to prostituting myself to get money to buy what I needed.

One day I woke up in a really bad place mentally. The night before I got beaten to a pulp from a "client" and I was in pain everywhere. I just didn't want to deal with life anymore. I was so sick of everything, of where my life was. Suddenly, the idea of carbon monoxide poisoning popped into my head, like the devil himself put it there.

I started to plan it out. In fact, it became like a puzzle, this piece goes here and that piece goes there and voila, succes! The puzzle is completed. Success, of course, was me dying. But when you start going down this road you don't really look at it like that anymore. You look at it as a mission to be finished.

The devil had control of me at this point. I no longer thought at it as a suicide, it was like a grocery list and I'm checking off the items one by one. You've completely removed yourself, your *life, your very being,* from what you are about to do. It's weird. Like you are not part of the plan, just the orchestrator of it.

I had the plan all laid out and I was ready to go, again the idea of dying and never breathing again, never saying hi to someone, never listening to a good song was completely removed from my thought process. It was all business, all about accomplishing the job at hand.

A couple of days later, I had the plan all laid out. I was about to head to the hardware store to buy the hose in which to pipe the carbon monoxide into this vehicle I had access to. This was going to be the day. I was determined. I figured it'd take no more than 2 hours from start to finish.

Then, all of a sudden, I heard the words 'It's going to be okay.' I literally heard this. Was it in my head or an actual voice? I don't know. But I heard the words and then this peace came over me like something I had never felt before. It was incredible. And just like that," Rachel snapped her fingers for emphasis. "The devil's spell was broken. He was leading me to my own demise and I had no clue it was happening! I still shudder when I think about how close I actually was to doing it. But The Holy Spirit intervened and sent the devil running. Why did He choose me? I'll never know. But I survived the devil's evil plan for me that day. Hallelujah!

Then, I had this feeling that I had to make it back to Peaks because God had a mission for me there. I had no money. No job. I was an addict. I was a pure mess. But now I had a *purpose*. And having a purpose for one's life changes everything.

"Somehow, I came into contact with the owner of *this* house," Rachel gestured at the house around her. "Ms. Grant was a sweet old lady who needed some help but more than anything, she needed companionship. She knew of my background and yet she still invited me to move in with her and essentially do the things she couldn't anymore. Cook, clean, remove snow, mow, the whole thing. She had no family. She needed me and I needed her. I like to think God brought us together. She literally saved my life.

Unfortunately, when I moved here, my reputation came with me so people here don't like me much. To top it off, because Ms. Grant left her house to me folks think I am a grifter who took advantage of her. They also see me as trying to change things on the island and they don't like that at all. I don't blame them though because while I'm not a grifter I *am* trying to change things on the island."

One More Day

"How long have you been clean now?" Rob asked.

"Over five years, I'm happy to say. It was in my first year of sobriety when I met Ms. Grant and came back to the island. She died a couple years ago, left me the house and I've been on my mission ever since. What I do now is give lectures for addicts and folks who are dealing with suicidal thoughts. I ask them to hang in there, for just one more day, just break that spell that has taken hold of you. The devil has tricked you as he tricked me. Just hang in for one more day. One More Day is the name of my talk, by the way.

Sadly, we've lost many. But we've saved some too and that makes it all worthwhile. Especially when the ones we've saved go on to have their own children. I can't tell you the joy. It's God's grace, no two ways around it."

"But if people around here see the good you're doing, why are they still hostile to you?" Rob asked.

"They think I'm part of a religious cult that's recruiting people and it scares them."

"A religious cult?" Rob scoffed. "You? Now don't take this wrong, Rachel but it's awful hard to see you as leading a cult. What are you like, 5'3" maybe 110 pounds!" Rob said laughing.

Rachel nodded. "I know it! But since Ms. Grant died there have been people such as yourself coming back to the island to check things out. People who hadn't been here in decades. They aren't coming during tourist season either. It's like we have been called here. I can't explain it. But the locals take notice and ask questions. And to be honest, I *am* recruiting people but not for a religious cult. I'm recruiting people who need a clean break from the chaos in their lives, to start fresh and the people who have taken over the island don't like that. They want Peaks to be like a Martha's Vineyard in Maine, free from the rabble, an exclusive place for the elite.

Now here I come, the farthest thing from the elite set, a poor junkie, and I'm encouraging others to come here and start fresh too, to rebuild. They *hate* me for that. I'm trying to bring the rabble they want to keep away!"

"So you're the outcast among the newly arrived in the very place you were raised. That's ironic if ever there was any irony. What do you think it is with this sudden draw, this pull for people to come back to Peaks? Seems almost supernatural." Rob asked.

"It *is* supernatural. Can I prove it? Of course not. But, yet, here you are. And again you're not the only one who has come back and sat in that exact chair you are in now. Do you remember Jeff Jamison?"

"Of course I do," Rob responded. "He and I were real good friends growing up but I haven't spoken to him since I left the island."

"Well, he became a big commercial real estate broker in the Boston area, *huge* as a matter of fact. He is worth millions, can you believe that?" Rachel chuckled at the thought.

In disbelief Rob said, "Jeff? Jeff Jamison became rich? No way! He was such a slouch growing up. No ambition at all."

"I know!" Rachel answered. "Crazy right? But something must have gone right because he has his own private plane, vacation homes on the Cape and in South Carolina. He was divorced but remarried to a cute, young thing who came out here with him. When I asked what brought him back to Peaks he said he had a weird dream that basically told him to come back. He didn't say much more than that though.

Unfortunately, when he was here I could tell he was not impressed with me, my story or even the idea he was being pulled back to the island. In fact, he was quite hostile. It was weird. You could see that he had spent his whole life building up financial assets and desperately wanted to forget his past as a poor boy on Peaks Island. It was like he was living the life rich people were supposed to live and he was never going back.

"Brian Joseph? Do you remember him?" Rachel asked.

"I remember Brian too!" Rob said excitedly. "Crazy how all these names bring me back. He was a short, heavier kid with thick glasses. Always kind of a mama's boy."

"Yup, that's him," Rachel said. "He is married, no kids. Lives in the Chicago area and owns a small plumbing business."

"Wait!" Rob said incredulously. "Brian? Brian Joseph owns a plumbing business? In Chicago? Now I've heard it all."

"Not only that but his wife, Isabella, is beautiful and she loves him dearly," said Rachel. "They are just the sweetest couple too. Brian's physical condition isn't good though. His body has taken a beating with his line of work and he is pretty heavy. Isabella is very worried about him so when he got the pull, so to speak, to come back and visit Peaks she encouraged him because of his health. She definitely liked it here but he was hesitant. He was so worried about their finances, even though they seem to be quite well off. But it's hard to let go if you're used to a certain lifestyle.

When they got back to Chicago he emailed me thanking me profusely for my hospitality but said he isn't going to come back. More than anything else he wants to make sure he doesn't leave Isabella broke if his physical condition continues to deteriorate. So, he'll keep working. Probably until he's dead. He just thinks he'll never have enough money. And yet it's his work that will probably kill him. It's quite sad."

Rob sighed and shook his head. "The worry about finances haunts *so* many people. It's like the more we get the more we worry. Is it really worth it?"

"Hard to say," Rachel responded. "I'm sure there are some folks who are high-spenders and are having a blast. I just know that's not a great way to live if you're piling on debt. On the other hand, Brian and Isabella had no debt and yet he was still worried about money, really for no reason at all."

She continued, "There are others who've come back to take a look too. It's actually pretty amazing. I have been able to recruit one person to move here so far. Her name is Janie McMillan. She's a few years younger than us and moved off the island when she was only like three or four, so I doubt you'd know her.

Her story is interesting. She lived in Portland, had kids, was "happily" married on the outside, but it was all pretend. Her whole life she covered up the fact she was gay. She thought if she forced herself to be "normal" by getting married and then having kids, things would get better. That didn't happen. She was miserable and every day was getting more desperate, to the point she was thinking it would be best to take her own life.

Then she met some folks who allowed her to be who she was. She started living a secret life and for the first time in her life she thought she was happy. But she had this incredible guilt of not being truthful with her husband and kids. The guilt wore on her until she began using. And then she couldn't stop. As is always the case, her addiction eventually caught up to her. Her husband left and was able to secure custody of the two kids. That sent her deep into the depths of hell.

Wasn't too long after the divorce that she ran out of money and she *also* took to prostituting herself to get the cash to feed *her* addiction. It's crazy how many "normal" women are out here doing this just to get cash for dope. Pretty soon she was living on the streets, not caring what she put in her body. If it killed her, so be it. She was a junkie with nothing to live for.

One day she woke up in a hospital after nearly dying from an overdose when she heard that Divine voice comforting her, telling her to clean herself up and move away. She asked her ex-husband for some money to help get situated in Nashua, New Hampshire. He was reluctant as he was worried she'd just use it for dope. But for the kids, and the hope that one day they'd see her clean again, he gave her the money. She moved down there, got a job through a temp agency which became a full-time gig and has been clean ever since, over three years now.

After visiting Portland to see her kids she attended one of my presentations and knew she had to help. We've developed a real close relationship since then," Rachel paused, looked at Rob and added, "if you know what I mean." She waited to see if there was any reaction on Rob's part. Rob nodded knowingly, so Rachel continued.

"She works remotely, which can be done on the island now. So she decided to make the move back to Peaks to live with me and support what I'm doing. She's actually giving a talk in town today, as a matter of fact, which is why she isn't here now. I can't tell you how exciting it is for me to have her with me. It was tough doing this alone but God provides, in His time, of course. So, now there are two of us. Of course, we're not a traditional family by any stretch of the imagination but the way I look at it, neither was Paul, or Peter, or any of the apostles. *Someone* has got to be the spark for which the fire can be built."

Then Rachel said no more. They both just sat there in their own thoughts, not an awkward silence but more like a couple who have been married for decades with no need to interrupt the quiet.

After a bit, Rachel suddenly asked, "are you happy, Rob?" Rob's head snapped back as he was taken aback by the question.

"What do you mean am I happy?"

"Pretty much what I asked, are you happy?" Rachel repeated. Rob was suspicious of such a question.

"I'm not sure what my happiness has to do with anything," he responded.

"Come on, Rob. Think about it. If you were happy and content in your life would you actually be here, on Peaks, without your family?

"Look Rachel, my life certainly isn't perfect. I admit that. I just know that when I heard about Marcus Simone dying it opened a floodgate of memories I hadn't thought about in years. I had to investigate what caused him to do that and it scares me to think about. What if I'm next? What if I become so distraught I take my own life and leave my kids without a dad? That's why I had to see if anyone had information as to what caused Marcus to kill himself. Was it a slow, gradual decline or did he just wake up one day and do it? Could he have stopped it if he had help or what? Maybe a change in scenery? I just knew that I needed to get away and for some reason Peaks was calling for me, just like the others you mentioned. It's weird."

"I'm not so sure it's that weird, Rob," Rachel replied. "Maybe it's a mid-life crisis or maybe it's an unseen force, God even, calling out to you? I don't know. I just know *my* life is better now being back on Peaks because I'm making a difference in the lives of others. I have a purpose for the first time in my life.

Maybe what's missing in your life is a true purpose, you're supposed to do something different with your life and Peaks Island is *where* you're supposed to be. Maybe there is a reason your parents moved here all those years ago and your mom stayed here to raise you.

Maybe the island is part of who you are and you need to come back."

When Rob didn't respond Rachel asked, "are you familiar with the Parable of the Talents, Rob?"

Rob replied, a bit defensively. "Of course I am, Rachel. Are you implying that I'm just burying my talents? Too afraid to take a risk? You *do* realize I'm raising children? Now, you don't have kids so you probably don't know all the work involved but let me tell you, it's a chore and it's not cheap. So, you could say my kids are my, uh, shall we say, 'talents.'"

"Interesting," Rachel replied back and said no more.

This conversation definitely wasn't going the way Rob had intended. He just wanted to know what happened to Marcus Simone after all.

"I still don't understand how you can not see this." Rachel said.

"See what?" Rob was curt. "I have no clue what you're talking about."

"Okay, let me spell it out for you. You're saying your kids are your legacy to the world. I completely agree. But could it be possible that right now you're raising your kids to follow in your footsteps… to take on debt and go work in a soulless job to pay it back? The typical American corporate grind where no one is actually content or happy. Maybe you've been so focused on your work you've lost those deep connections to your own family. Could it be that the reason you're here is the island's way of calling you back? To help you rebuild your relationship with your family?"

Rob laughed a bit mockingly. "You act like "the island" is some living thing. Come on, Rachel. That just sounds crazy."

"It is crazy, Rob! But you can't tell me the world around you isn't crazy too! Everyone's world seems to have gone crazy. Yet, it doesn't take much to change worlds, and obviously yours needs changing or else you wouldn't be here to begin with."

"Change the world?" Rob laughed. "Seems pretty far-fetched. Like I said before, the only reason I'm here is because I'm trying to find out why Marcus Simone killed himself. Nothing more than that."

"I didn't say "change the world", did I?" Rachel quickly retorted. "My exact words were "change worlds.""

Rob scoffed. "Same thing."

"No! it's not, Rob!" She responded vociferously. Rob was actually taken aback at her ferocity. "Changing worlds is changing individual people, *their* worlds get changed, from the inside! It happens when they realize they're not alone, that there are people who know what they're going through and are there to help."

Rachel then softened her tone. "Once you've experienced that change in yourself you want to be there for others who are desperate to change as well. You are literally changing worlds, one human being at a time."

Rachel paused and took a deep breath. "When *you* have been healed on the inside, you can't help but to try to pull people out of that black hole of desperation and loneliness that they're in because you know if *you* can be rescued from the despair so can they. But you've got to fix yourself first."

After an awkward silence Rob asked, "okay, I get it. This is very important to you. But what does that have to do with me?"

"What does it have to do with you? Are you serious? You're here investigating why Marcus killed himself, no? You don't see the connection? You know your corporate life is starting to grind on you, driving a wedge between you and your family. And even worse, you're starting to worry about your own emotional state. You're worried you'll do something similar to Marcus and leave your kids to pick up the pieces. And you obviously have this feeling you need to change before it's too late.

Out here, in our small community, you can change. And best of all, you can show your kids there is a different way forward than what they've seen from you so far. You can have a purpose!

And even better is that the island where you grew up needs you too. It needs you to save it from the soulless who are taking over. It needs kids. It needs its school. It needs families to bring back the community that has been lost. Your family could be the beacon for others to come and join us. To re-energize this place with the sound of children's giggles.

And *you* need it too. You were not put on this world to 'get by' at some job you don't like just for money. You were put on this world to thrive, to invest your talents so when you return back to God He will say 'Well done, good and faithful servant.'"

Rob was incredulous. "Whoa. That's a lot of responsibility to put on me, Rachel. So it's *my* family that's going to save this place? Seems like a task well beyond my ability."

Rachel became exasperated again. "Rob, it's not just you! The Divine Hand is at work here. You and I and others are just the tools being used to implement God's work. Think about it. Go back to when your mom moved here. All that she went through to find her way here. You think everything that happened over two generations is mere coincidence?"

"You know an awful lot about my family, Rachel." Rob stated. "It's kind of creepy."

"I already told you, I've been snooping. I've missed too many opportunities and I'm not sure how many more chances I'll get. So, knowing that you were coming out, I had to give you my best sales pitch. Which meant a lot of research." Rachel responded and laughed a bit as she said it.

She continued. "Here's the way I see it. And you can take it or leave. Call me crazy. Whatever. When the other people came to see me I was too timid to let them know what I think was happening here. So I'm just going to be blunt with you, Rob. The way I see it is that modern America has lost its soul in pursuit of material things. When the sense of community is removed, people get lost. They seek relief in the temporary things that money buys, gimmicks essentially. These things never satisfy the need for what is missing, though. In forever chasing fulfillment, emptiness sets in and eventually hopelessness.

Being part of a community is to be human. Trying to go it alone is not natural and is, well, I think killing people. I mean just look at what happened to Marcus. But it's not just him. Suicide is rising dramatically in this country among people in their 50s and even 60s. Why is that?

Think about it, when was the last time you sent a kid to your neighbors house to get a cup of sugar because you ran out? Never! Now you just get in your car and go to the local grocery story. But while that may be convenient, it's *not* community. In fact, convenience further insulates us and removes us even more from the human interaction we need. It is getting even worse now because of computers and smartphones. It's robotic and inhuman. We are truly losing our humanity. Crazy isn't it? It's so obvious when you take a moment to think about it. Human beings need each other and yet we are moving further apart into isolation.

"So now you've got middle-aged, financially successful people who are completely lost. While the material rewards they've attained are large, they are poor, poor in the soul. Poverty of the soul leads to despair and ultimately to destruction.

I literally think there is a natural force of some kind that's beginning to push back. This force, God is what I think It is, is warning people to embrace their humanity again. That is what Marcus Simone's death was…a warning to you to change before it's too late."

What Next?

Rob looked at Rachel, about to lie and say that he *was* doing just fine, that this was all just a coincidence after all. But she could see right through him. The look on her face said it all, 'stop lying to yourself'. Rob looked away, embarrassed, and stared out the open window which allowed the crispness of the October island breeze to flow through the house. The sun had set and the island had become dark and quiet. No rush hour commuters with their honking horns. Just the gentle ringing of buoys floating in Casco Bay and the fainting sounds of seagulls trying to catch their last meal before settling in for the night. Peace. Just peace.

Suddenly, the thought of his kids crept into his mind. Did he really want them to continue to be raised by an absentee dad? A dad on the gerbil wheel chasing the carrot being waved in front of him. "Just a bit more, Rob...just another lap. Keep it up and you'll have a seven-figure retirement portfolio! Keep going and you can even buy a beautiful vacation home! Keep at it and happiness will come!"

But wait, why did any of that matter if the people who were most dear to him, his wife and kids, were the sacrifice? A vacation home, a large retirement account, all the money in the world meant nothing if the people he loved were not there to share it with him.

He remembered Ed, a client of his he'd visit a couple times a year in New York City. Ed was in his mid 70's and wealthy. He lived in a fancy brownstone in Manhattan. He seemed to have it all. Except he didn't. He lived alone. He lost his family in his quest for more financial accumulation. His one piece of advice to Rob was to "always be home for dinner. That's what I didn't realize until it was too late. Now I'm retired, I'm wealthy and I'm alone. My family is gone." How had Rob forgotten this?

And then Sandy. What had he done to that poor girl? She was there when times were so tight, when they had their first kid and were worried where the money was going to come from to pay the bills. It was tough times but Rob wouldn't trade those moments for the world. Those were the times that made them a team, Sandy and Rob facing the world together. And they did it! They won. But what exactly was the prize? This lifestyle they now had was driving them apart. That was a pyrrhic victory if ever there was one. You finally make it to the top but when you get there you're all alone, like Ed. Yeah, what a victory.

Right then Rob knew what he had to do. Nothing had ever been so clear to him. "Rachel, would you excuse me for a moment? I've got to call my wife and save my marriage." Rachel nodded as Rob stepped outside onto the front porch.

He retrieved the cellphone out of his pocket and prayed that he'd get coverage here. He needed to talk to Sandy and right now. This was urgent. Maybe more urgent than anything he had ever done in his life. He looked at the bars and there were three. Should be enough to reach her. Will she pick up? Please pick up Sandy. Please… One ring, two, three, nothing. Rob's heart sank. Four rings… it's over, he thought to himself. I'm too late. Just when I had clarity too. Man, how did I screw this up, *again*??? Five rings… Rob was about to hang up, when, "yes Rob…" It was Sandy. She sounded exasperated, disappointed even. There was noise in the background and Rob realized she was at the Club with her friends. The next words out of Rob's mouth might be the most important things he'd ever say.

"Sandy, I love you. I've been so, so stupid. I know it now. So, let's start over, can we? Let's sell the house and move. I'll get a different job where I won't be away from the family. Let's go back to the way it was when the kids were first born. Except this time we'll have some money in the bank. What do you say?"

There was a pause. Rob's heart stopped. Nothing. He heard nothing but background noise and then a deep breath from Sandy. Rob braced for impact. He wasn't sure he'd be able to handle it if Sandy rejected him.

Then Sandy began to speak. "Rob," she said softly. Rob couldn't breathe. "I thought you'd never ask."

It took a moment before Rob could process what he had heard. Then, he couldn't hold back; he started to cry. "Thank you, Sandy. Thank you." He dropped to his knees, thanked the Lord and he cried some more.

The screen door behind him creaked as it opened. Rachel stood there under the soft porchlight, a smile as bright as the sun in the clearest summer sky in Maine spread across her face. One More Day, she thought and silently thanked the Lord herself for allowing redemption.

Conclusion

While the backstory of this story is liberally based on my life growing up in Maine it is still a work of complete fiction. For anyone who knows me, do not make more out of this than that. It's just a story.

But there IS a message I wanted to convey, nonetheless. That message is to enjoy your life with your family TODAY. Do not get so caught up in the chasing of material things that you forget what is most important after God, your family!

The "Ed" who makes a brief appearance in this story is a real person, by the way. I met with him for lunch one day in Manhattan. He was a client of mine, retired, a couple million in his portfolio, no debt and living in the city. I'll never forget those words he shared with me, "always be at home for dinner." It was a warning to me and let me share it as a warning for you too. You were not put on this earth to slave away at some crappy, old job regardless of the financial rewards. You were put on this earth to love one another and do good things to help your fellow man.

So then, how do you go about it? Man, oh man, I can't tell you that. I've no clue what your situation is. Hopefully, you're not carrying huge debt. Debt is the Devil's work. It keeps you from doing what God wants you to do. It truly makes one an indentured servant.

In fact, in Romans 13:8 Paul states it so well…
"Let no debt remain outstanding, except the continuing debt to love one another, for whoever loves others has fulfilled the law." And of course we know from Proverbs "the borrower is slave to the lender."

The point is that if you've accumulated debt you're limited what you can do with what God has blessed you with. Maybe you want to take in abandoned dogs, train them and give them to families who need a service animal. Hard to do if half your paycheck is currently going to service your debt.

Maybe you want to move to a cheaper part of the country where a dollar goes further, hard to do if you're upside down on your home mortgage. How are you going to pay that off if you have no equity?

So, the first thing to strive for is to remove that albatross of debt off of your neck. Until that's been slayed, you're still at the whim of the lender.

Now, let's say debt is no longer an issue. First off, congratulations to you. You're off to do great, great things for humanity. But what will that be? I don't know. But you know Who knows? God. And He will tell you. But you have to be open to hear Him speak to you.

Which means you need to put down all your devices, anything that distracts you, and just take a bit of time each day, 15 minutes maybe is all you need, to sit, in the quiet and listen. I'm telling you, try this. Just wake up in the morning. Get a cup of coffee and just SIT

THERE! Do not check your phone. Do NOTHING. Literally, nothing. Just sit there and let the quiet engulf you. This is when you're ripe to hear God's words. It's truly amazing what you'll hear.

The Devil hates the silence. Because he knows it's in that silence you're hearing God. The Devil LOVES noise. Just like C.S. Lewis said in The Screwtape Letters:

Music and silence–how I detest them both!....[Hell] has been occupied by Noise–Noise, the grand dynamism, the audible expression of all that is exultant, ruthless, and virile–Noise which alone defends us from silly qualms, despairing scruples and impossible desires. We will make the whole universe a noise in the end....The melodies and silences of Heaven will be shouted down in the end. (The Screwtape Letters, 119-120)

My guidance to you as you consider the next path in your life is to listen to the silence. Allow God to speak His words to you. It may take time. But listen. Every day, just listen…

Oh, and stay out of debt.

Blessings,

Josh Scandlen
Milton, GA June 2022

9 7 9 8 8 3 3 9 6 7 0 8 9